"I don't confuse my senses and my heart."

"Don't you?" Raschid challenged softly. Felicia trembled under the deliberate provocation of his caresses, and he laughed deep in his throat.

"And what do your senses tell you now, Miss Gordon?"

It was too late to pretend that his touch left her unaffected, too late by far. "They tell me that sex without love is like the desert without water—an arid wasteland where nothing can flourish."

He bent his head toward her, and Felicia was like the falcon's prey, transfixed, accepting her fate.

"Have you experienced the potency of the desert, Miss Gordon?"

With an anguished cry she tore herself free. Was he trying to seduce her away from Faisal? Faisal! Why had the memory of his love not protected her from responding to Raschid?

PENNY JORDAN

falcon's prey

Harlequin Books

TORONTO • LONDON • LOS ANGELES • AMSTERDAM
SYDNEY • HAMBURG • PARIS • STOCKHOLM • ATHENS • TOKYO

Harlequin Presents edition published December 1981
ISBN 0-373-10471-5

Original hardcover edition published in 1981
by Mills & Boon Limited

CHAPTER ONE

THE restaurant was well known and expensive, and Felicia had to pretend to be unaware of the waiter's contemptuous appraisal of her shabby coat as she hurriedly surveyed the occupants of the tables.

Her spirits lifted when she saw Faisal, and the waiter, plainly reviewing his opinion of her when he saw with whom she was to dine, cleared a path for her with an alacrity which she secretly found amusing. It spoke volumes for the power of money, she reflected, as Faisal pushed back his chair and stood up, an appreciative smile lighting his handsome features.

'I'm sorry I'm so late,' she apologised as they sat down. 'I was late leaving the office.'

'The office! Zut! Have I not told you before to give up this worthless job?' Faisal demanded with an arrogance that slightly dismayed her.

An attractive girl, with auburn hair that curled on to her shoulders and sombre green eyes that hinted at a natural reserve, Felicia was unaware of the assessing glances of some of the other diners. Although her neat ribbed sweater and toning tweed skirt instantly placed her apart from the elegant creatures in silks and furs who sat at the other tables, she had a lissom grace which automatically drew the male eye.

That Faisal was aware of this was obvious from the jealous looks he gave these other men who dared to look upon his Felicia; but Felicia herself was completely unaware of the slight stir caused by her entrance.

She had known the young Kuwaiti for just six breathless weeks. A mutual interest in photography had led to their initial meeting at night school classes and one or two casual dates had grown into regular thrice weekly meetings, and more latterly dates most nights of the week as Faisal grew increasingly possessive.

With Faisal's insistence that he take her out to lunch most days of the week, and dates nearly every night as well, it had proved impossible to keep their romance a secret from the other girls in her office. At first they had teased her unmercifully, until they realised that the affair was becoming serious. Then their lighthearted teasing had turned to warnings of a more serious nature as they repeated direful tales of what could happen to European girls foolish enough to take the promises of rich Middle Eastern males too seriously. Felicia kept her own counsel. She was sure that Faisal respected her too much to hurt her in the way that they were suggesting, but even so, she had been surprised and then flattered when he began to talk about marriage.

During these talks he had told her a good deal about his family, just as she had told him about her parents, dying so young and so tragically when she was little more than a baby, and leaving her to be brought up by Aunt Ellen and Uncle George in their bleak granite house on the Lancashire moors.

Her childhood had not been a happy one. Uncle George had been a strict and unbending guardian, whose constant rejection had built up in her a lack of self-confidence coupled with the feeling that in failing to gain his love she had somehow failed as a human being. Consequently, in the warmth of Faisal's readily expressed adoration she had begun to bloom like a plant brought out of the frost into a tropical conservatory.

Faisal's stories of his own childhood enchanted her, and she often reflected upon how fortunate he had been to be brought up surrounded by the love of his mother and sisters. If only she too might have been part of such a happy family!

She readily admitted that Faisal had swept her off her feet. They had not known one another nearly long enough, she protested when he talked beguilingly of marriage, but Faisal swept aside her protests. They were made for one another. How could she deny it? How could she, when he wrapped her in the protective warmth of his love? She had said nothing of this to the girls at work. Faisal merely wanted her as a playmate to while away his time in London before returning home to make a 'good' marriage, arranged by his family, they warned her, but Felicia knew that this was not so.

She and Faisal were not lovers. He had been at first reproachful, and then approving of her refusal to give in to his pleas that she spend her nights with him as well as her days.

Her refusal had nothing to do with being prudish, or a calculated holding out for something more permanent than an affair. The truth was that Felicia was half frightened of such as yet unknown intimacies. In her teenage years Uncle George had been far too strict to permit her to indulge in the usual sexual experimentation of her peers, and as she had grown older she had developed a fastidious hesitancy about committing herself to any purely physical relationship. The first time Faisal had kissed her, he had been gentle, and almost reverent. But more lately, as his desire for her increased, Felicia had to confess to a feeling of nervous, spiralling alarm. And yet what was there to be afraid of? she chided herself. Faisal loved her. He had said so on many, many occasions, and she had agreed to be his wife. At first she had been anxious in case her inexperience made him turn to another, more willing girl, but to her surprise he seemed to approve of her hesitancy, even while he railed against it.

'It will be different once we are married,' he had soothed one evening when his emotions had threatened to get out of control, and Felicia had moaned a small protest at the passion of his kiss, but she had been comforted by his words. Even now she could hardly believe that someone actually loved *her*. After all, she reflected humbly, there was nothing special about her; thousands of girls had creamy skin and red-gold hair; and thousands more had slender, elegant bodies; she was nothing out of the ordinary.

Faisal told her that she was far too modest. He told her that her eyes were as green as an oasis after rain, and her hair the colour of molten sand as the dying rays of the sun scorched it. He likened her body to the movement of a falcon in flight, and told her that with her milk-white skin and soft, vulnerable mouth she was his heart's delight.

Already, despite her protests, he had bought her a ring—a flashing emerald to match her eyes, and so patently valuable that when she saw it Felicia had caught her breath in dismay.

Ten days ago Faisal had written to his family in Kuwait telling them of his intentions. Over the weeks Felicia had heard a good deal about Faisal's family—his mother and two sisters, the life they led, but most of all Faisal had talked about his uncle, who, upon the death of Faisal's father, had become the head of their household. Although it was never said directly, Felicia sensed that there existed a certain amount of constraint between Faisal and his uncle, and guessed that the older man did not always approve of the actions of the younger.

Felicia already knew that through his mother and uncle, Faisal was related to the ruling family of Kuwait and that this uncle had done much for the bereaved family, even to the extent of taking them into his own home and undertaking all the responsibility for the education of Faisal and his sisters.

The tribe to which Faisal belonged had come originally from the desert; fierce, proud warriors with a long history of tribal warfare and bloodshed. As recently as the lifetime of Faisal's great-grandfather the tribes had waged war upon one another, and Faisal had confided to Felicia that his uncle's grandmother had been an English girl, plucked from the desert by a hawk-eyed chieftain whose prompt action had probably saved her life. She was the daughter of an explorer, Faisal went on to explain, and as a reward for his timely rescue the desert chieftain had claimed the hand of his pale-skinned hostage in marriage.

Privately Felicia thought the story unbelievably romantic. She had longed to ask Faisal more about the couple, and found it vaguely comforting to know that there was already English blood running through the veins of the family into which she would be marrying.

Nowadays Faisal's family no longer roamed the desert, for Faisal's maternal grandfather had founded a merchant bank at the time that oil was first discovered in Kuwait, and now that bank had offices in New York and London, ruling a financial empire so vast and complex that Felicia's head spun whenever Faisal tried to explain its workings to her. As he had also told her, and not without a hint of annoyance, this empire was directly controlled by his uncle, who was the majority shareholder, and who, therefore, had the power to manipulate Faisal, as an employee, very much like a pawn on a chessboard.

That Faisal should find this irksome, Felicia could well understand. She too had suffered from the dictatorial attitude of an unkind guardian. However, some of Faisal's sulky observances concerning his uncle she was inclined to take with a pinch of salt. Faisal was an extremely wealthy young man, by anyone's standards, kept short of nothing that would make his life more comfortable, and if his uncle was insisting that he learn the ropes of their business from the bottom upwards, so to speak, wasn't this, in the long run, a sensible method of preparing him for the responsibility which would one day be his?

However, today Faisal seemed more inclined than usual to complain about his uncle, and sudden uneasy intuition made Felicia ask anxiously:

'Have you heard something from Kuwait, Faisal?'

His dark eyes flashed angrily, reminding her for a moment how very young he was—barely twelve months older than her.

'My uncle thinks we should wait before announcing our engagement,' he admitted at last. 'He is doing this deliberately. He does not want me to be happy.'

'But we have only known one another a short time,' Felicia soothed. 'And it's not as though your family know me at all. Naturally they must be anxious.' She broke off to stare at Faisal, wondering what had changed his anger suddenly to excitement. 'What have I said?' she asked in bewilderment.

'It is nothing—just that you voiced Uncle Raschid's own doubts. You have never met my family and because of this he would have us delay our engagement, but I have thought of a way to outwit him, my Felicia, and force him to admit that he is wrong when he says that East and West cannot live in harmony. In his letter my uncle suggests that you might go to Kuwait to see for yourself how we live. Oh, I know what is behind his invitation,' he added, before Felicia could speak. 'He thinks that you will refuse—that you are as those other European girls who flock around us like vultures to meat—but we shall prove him wrong, you and I. Once we are married there will be no need for us to spend much time in Kuwait, and Raschid knows this. Still he insists that you must accustom yourself to our ways. I know what is behind his thinking, but it will not work. Tell me you will go to Kuwait, Felicia, and prove him wrong in his assessment of you.'

Felicia was taken completely off guard. Whatever reaction she had expected from Faisal's family it was not this! It was becoming increasingly plain that Faisal's uncle did not want him to marry her. But why not? Didn't he consider her as worthy of Faisal as a Kuwaiti girl? The thought sparked off instant anger and her chin lifted proudly. If Faisal wanted her to go to Kuwait with him to prove to this uncle just how wrong he was, then she would.

'When are we to go?' she asked determinedly, dismayed when Faisal flushed slightly.

'I cannot go, Felicia,' he muttered. 'Uncle Raschid has given orders that I am to start work at the New York office in a week's time.'

Felicia could barely take it in. 'A week? But. . . .'

'Raschid is determined to part us,' Faisal announced bitterly. 'He knows I cannot ignore his command. Despite the fact that he is my uncle, I am only an employee until I get my shares—but that is not until I am twenty-five, another three years.'

'I could come to New York with you,' Felicia said eagerly, trying to find a way round Raschid's edict. 'I could get a job, I. . . .'

Faisal shook his head regretfully.

'It is not that simple, my lovely one. To get a job you would need a visa, which would not be easily forthcoming. Of course you could simply accompany me, but then Raschid will claim that you are my mistress, and my mother and sisters could then never acknowledge you. No . . .' he said bleakly, 'the only way is for you to convince Raschid that he is wrong, that you are not what he thinks you.' He grasped her hands, his eyes pleading, and Felicia felt her anger melting. 'Promise me you will go . . . for the sake of our future together. My mother will make you truly welcome, and Raschid will be forced to acknowledge his error.'

Unable to deny how pleasurable this prospect was, Felicia still frowned a little. Kuwait—a civilisation away. And yet if she refused . . . She would go! She would show Faisal's uncle that English girls could be just as chaste as those of his own race. She would show him just how worthy of Faisal's love she was! He was Uncle George all over again, she thought resentfully, rejecting her, casting her aside as though she were some sort of inferior being. Well, she would show him!

The rest of the meal passed in a daze for Felicia. A thousand questions clamoured for answers.

Not for one moment did she believe that Faisal's uncle cared about her accustoming herself to their ways—no, he merely wanted to prove to her how unsuitable she was to be Faisal's bride. Faisal himself had practically admitted as much. 'Raschid will never expect you to accept his invitation,' he said with a good deal of satisfaction, when Felicia conveyed her decision to him.

Invitation! Command, more like, Felicia thought wrathfully. A command to present herself for inspection and rejection. Well, for Faisal's sake she would 'present' herself, but not for one moment was Faisal's lordly uncle going to be allowed to think that he could pass judgment on her!

'Come back with me to my apartment,' Faisal begged her when they had finished eating. 'There is much I must tell you about my family and our ways. . . .'

Normally Felicia avoided being too much alone with Faisal, but tonight she did not demur, and in the taxi she plagued him with questions about his country.

'Shall I have to wear a veil or go into purdah?' she asked him anxiously.

Faisal shook his head.

'Of course not. The older generation still adhere to those ways, but nowadays our girls are well educated, part of the emancipation that has swept our country. You will love Kuwait, Felicia, as I do myself. Although I must confess that I also love London, for different reasons. . . .'

The sudden passion she saw flaring in his eyes made Felicia glad that the taxi had stopped. Faisal had an apartment in an expensive and exclusive Mayfair block, furnished with a modern décor of stark white walls and carpets, with plushy hide chesterfields in dark leather and a quantity of smoked glass coffee tables and matching display shelves. She admired the apartment, but found it too palatial and immaculate; too impersonal in its stark elegance.

Faisal's manservant greeted them, offering Felicia coffee which she refused, watching Faisal while he put a tape in the complex hi-fi system stacked in one corner of the huge room. The haunting and evocative sound of the Carpenters swept the room; Faisal pressed a button, instantly dimming the lights, the heavy off-white curtains shutting out their aerial view of London.

As he took her in his arms, Felicia felt herself stiffen slightly. Why couldn't she relax? she chided herself. Faisal meant her no harm. He was, after all, the man she was going to marry. What was the matter with her? Why could she not abandon herself to the passion she had heard other girls discussing so frankly?

'What is wrong?' Faisal whispered, unconsciously reiterating her own thoughts. 'You stiffen and tremble at my touch like a dove in the talons of a hawk,' he told her indulgently. 'When we are parted, I shall dream of the moment when I lift the gold necklace from your bridal caftan and unfasten the one hundred and one buttons, to discover the one thousand and one beauties of your body. Do not worry,' he assured her confidently, 'your reluctance is as it should be. You are as chaste as the milk-white doves my mother keeps in her courtyard, and soon my uncle shall know that for himself.'

There was a certain element of satisfaction in his words, but Felicia could not help trembling a little with fear. Faisal seemed so confident that once they were married she would respond with passion to his lovemaking, but what if this should not be so? What if she was incapable of passion? Although her heart thrilled to his words of love, her body felt only nervous fear. Faisal's desire for her was increased by his knowledge that she had had no other lover, she knew that. But what if this had not been so? Did he love her, or her chastity? She banished the thought as unworthy. This was undoubtedly an after-effect of Faisal's disclosure concerning his uncle. It was only natural that Faisal should place greater importance on purity in his bride than her own countrymen, it was part and parcel of his upbringing. And yet this admission served only to stir fresh doubts.

'It is just as well that I am not rich enough to support more than one of the four wives I am allotted by Allah,' Faisal murmured, alarming her still further, 'for with you in my arms I could want no other, Felicia.'

It was this knowledge to which she must cling in the

weeks ahead, Felicia reminded herself—not her own lack
of reaction to Faisal's lovemaking. It was only her inexperience that made her doubt her capacity for response.
However, his remark about the four wives permitted to
men of the Moslem faith had also disturbed her. It came
as a shock to remember that he came from a vastly different culture from her own; a culture that permitted a man
more than one wife as long as he was able to maintain
them all in equal comfort; a culture that made no pretence
of being anything other than male-orientated, and yet the
Arab women she had seen were always so serene, Felicia
acknowledged, so candidly appealing; so protected from all
the unpleasantness of life by their male relatives. There
was the other side to the coin, though; harsh punishments
for those women who went against the rulings of the
Koran, or so Felicia had read, and she could not in all
honesty picture herself as merely a dutiful plaything,
living only through her husband.

All at once the task ahead loomed ominously. If only
Faisal could accompany her to Kuwait, to ease those first
uncomfortable and uncertain days when she was still a
stranger to his family. How subtle his uncle had been,
suggesting this visit; more subtle than she had at first
realised. Although Faisal was a comparatively wealthy
young man, as he had told her, the bulk of his inheritance
was tied up in the family merchant banking empire, held
in trust for Faisal by his uncle until his twenty-fifth birthday. Until that time Faisal was virtually dependent upon
his uncle both for employment and finance. Discarding the
disloyal thought that Faisal could have got round his
uncle's edict simply by finding a job in England as totally
impractical, Felicia acknowledged uneasily that at present
it appeared that Faisal's uncle had the upper hand.

Here she was, virtually committed to journeying alone
to a strange country, forced to court the approval of a
man who, she was sure, was deliberately trying to force
her to show herself in a bad light, and would probably
never approve of their marriage.

'Are you sure your mother will like me, Faisal?' she asked in a small uncertain voice.

'She will love you as I do,' he promised. 'It will not be so bad, you will see. I am to spend two months in New York, and then we shall be together again. Then we shall make plans for our wedding. Perhaps it is as well that you will be with my family. That way no other man can cast covetous eyes upon you. You are mine, Felicia,' he told her arrogantly, unobservant of the faint shadows lingering in her eyes.

Faisal drove her back to her flat himself in the car he kept parked in the underground car-park provided for the use of the apartment tenants. It was an opulent Mercedes with cream leather upholstery and every refinement known to technological man, from a hidden cocktail cabinet to an in-car phone and a highly sophisticated hi-fi system.

Privately Felicia considered that Faisal drove too fast, but on the one occasion she had mentioned this to him he had looked so angry that she had not done so again.

'As you are a guest of my family, it is only right that we should pay all your expenses,' he told her when he stopped the car outside the small and rather shabby bedsit that had been her home since she first came to London.

Felicia protested, unwilling for Faisal's family to think of her as being financially grasping and reminding him that the knowledge that she had not paid for her own ticket would surely influence his uncle against her.

'He will not know,' he assured her carelessly, 'and besides, you will need some new clothes, more suitable for our climate.'

It struck Felicia that perhaps he feared that she would shame him with her small wardrobe, for she was aware of the importance his people placed upon outward show, and so, unwillingly, she allowed him to persuade her to accept the gift of her ticket and save her money for what he termed 'necessary expenditure'.

The days flew past, with her seeing Faisal every evening. She wanted to learn as much about the country she was going to as she could, and often by the time Faisal took her home her brain was a confused jumble of facts and figures.

Even so, she could not help but admire the tireless energy of the Kuwait Government when she learned just how much had been achieved in such a very short span of time.

Even allowing for the fact that the country's vast oil revenues had made many types of technological advancement possible, the swift transition from an almost medieval way of life to the twentieth century left her breathless.

Naturally Faisal was proud of his country's progress, the more so because his own family had had a large part in it. It was with great sincerity that he told Felicia of their democratic form of government, with the Head of State chosen from amongst the descendants of Sheikh Mubarak al Sabah, who had ruled the country from 1896 to 1915, and was, even now, referred to simply as 'Al Kebir'—The Great.

Although Faisal deliberately played the relationship down, Felicia was a little dismayed to learn that his family were distantly connected to the ruling house. Faisal assured her that she must not let this overwhelm her, but she was beginning to see why his Uncle Raschid might not approve of Faisal's choice of bride.

Naturally, she was fascinated by this glimpse into another world—albeit a very rich and exotic one; however, whenever she tried to voice her doubts as to her ability to cope with so many changes, Faisal merely laughed, telling her that his family would adore her.

'Even Raschid will be impressed by your beauty. You have the colouring of his grandmother,' he told her, eyeing her speculatively. 'You will surprise him with your innocence and modesty.'

Felicia could only pray that this was indeed so, pressing

Faisal to tell her a little more about his own background.

Nothing loath, he described to her the modern town of Kuwait, which had now taken the place of the old mud-brick port. His family had extensive financial interests in the new city—their bank had helped finance the erection of a modern hotel in which they held a controlling interest, and there were other buildings, office blocks, apartments, shipping interests; all of which made Felicia uneasily aware of the vast gap that lay between them.

Kuwait had one of the best social service systems in the world, Faisal boasted proudly, with excellent schooling, a hospital system that would have made a Harley Street surgeon pea-green with envy, low-cost housing for people at the bottom end of the social scale, and very much more. Felicia was properly impressed, but Faisal shrugged it all aside. 'Much is made possible by money,' he told her, 'But there is still the huge vastness of the desert, which Uncle Raschid claims will never be tamed. For myself I prefer London or New York, and it is in one of these cities that we shall make our home.'

Felicia was surprised that this should make her faintly sorry.

She noticed also that Faisal was at pains to assure her that although most Kuwaitis were adherents to the Moslem faith, there was no bias against people of other faiths; nor would she be expected to change her own religion when they married.

'That at least is something Uncle Raschid cannot hold against you,' he surprised her by saying, 'for although all of us are of the Moslem faith, because of the great love Raschid's grandfather bore his English wife, her descendants are of your faith, thus Uncle Raschid himself is a Christian.'

Christian or not, Felicia was not looking forward to making his acquaintance—especially without Faisal's comforting support. The eventual confrontation loomed unpleasantly on the horizon, but not wanting to burden

Faisal with her own worries, she kept her fears to herself, trying to ensure that their last few days together were as carefree as possible.

For Faisal's sake she would do all she could to make a good impression on his uncle, but her pride would not let her adopt the fawning attitude of a Moslem women to an older male relative—no matter how he might disapprove of her independence!

With her seat booked, she handed in her notice at work, and carefully scoured the shops for suitable clothes. Fortunately the early summer fashions were already on display and she had no trouble at all in buying half a dozen pretty cotton dresses and pastel-toned separates.

She hesitated over the purchase of beach clothes, but as Faisal had told her that the beaches off Failaka Island and the surrounding coast were particularly beautiful, she succumbed to the lure of the matching apple-green towelling set of shorts, bikini and jacket. Egged on by the assistant, she added another bikini in swirling blues and greens which complemented her eyes, and a plain black swimsuit for good measure, unaware that its skilful cut emphasised the slender length of her legs and the unexpectedly full curve of her breasts. One evening dress in palest Nile green silk completed her new wardrobe, and although she could barely afford it, Felicia could not deny that the slender slip of fabric was infinitely becoming, tiny diamanté straps supporting the swathed bodice, the skirt falling in folds to whisper seductively round slender legs. Her purchases complete, she allowed herself the luxury of a taxi back to her small bedsit. Faisal was taking her out to dinner and as it would be their last evening together, she wanted to look her best.

As she put away her new clothes, her eyes alighted on the jewellers' box which contained the emerald he had bought her. Only the previous evening they had quarrelled because she refused to wear it until their engagement had the sanction of his family. He has teased her about being old-fashioned, but she sensed that to flaunt the opu-

lent stone before his uncle would immediately set his back
up. She suspected that the older man would hold rigid
and old-fashioned views on such subjects, and while she
intended in no way to kow-tow to him, she had no wish
to deliberately offend against his opinions.

Even so, it was hard not to feel bitter about his obvious
contempt of her—contempt he had expressed overtly in
his letter to Faisal, and this without knowing the first
thing about her! Perhaps it was this bitterness that made
her more reckless than usual, choosing to wear a dress which
had hung unworn in her wardrobe ever since she had
bought it, deeming it too sophisticated and eye-catch-
ing.

She had purchased it at the insistence of the colleague
with whom she had gone shopping, and afterwards had
regretted the impulsive buy, deeming it more suitable for
the baby blue eyes and blonde curls of her friend than
herself. Not that she had anything against the colour as
such. The dress was black, which she knew suited her
creamy skin, but it was low-cut, with a pencil-slim skirt,
slit up one side to reveal slim thighs, its design emphasising
her curves to a degree which made her feel acutely self-
conscious. It was just the sort of dress Faisal's uncle would
expect a gold-digging girl to choose, she acknowledged
wryly as she zipped it up, and she was in two minds
whether or not to change it when she heard Faisal's knock
on the door.

His eyes smouldered with desire when she went to let
him in, and she was glad of the long-sleeved jacket which
went with the dress, although she could not help noticing
how the matt black fabric made her auburn hair seem
much more vivid than usual, darkening her eyes to a
slumbrous, mysterious jade.

Faisal himself looked extremely smart, dressed in a
plum velvet dinner suit—affected on anyone else, but
somehow on him exactly right—his complexion somehow
more olive and Eastern so that she was immediately
reminded of the vast gulf in their cultures.

'I wish we were eating in my apartment—alone—and not in a restaurant where I must share your beauty with others,' Faisal murmured huskily, capturing her hands.

She tensed as he kissed her, telling herself that with their parting so very imminent it was no wonder that she felt so nervous. Even so, she was glad when he released her, bending to help her into her fake fur jacket.

'Why will you not let me buy you a proper fur?' he grumbled as he led the way to his car. 'You are very stubborn and foolish. Remember that once you are my wife I shall have the power to compel you to accept whatever gifts I choose to bestow upon you.'

'Then you may buy me as many fur coats as you please,' Felicia retorted lightly, wishing she could throw off the childhood training which prevented her from responding to him as lovingly as she would have wished.

Faisal, however, seemed to notice nothing amiss in her response. Felicia knew that he would have bought her the sun, the moon and all the stars if she let him, but she had no intention of accepting expensive gifts from him before their marriage. She knew from listening to his friends' conversation what the Arab community thought of the British girls who gave their favours so freely in return for a diamond bracelet or a fur, and she wondered if those same girls had the slightest idea of the contempt in which they were held by their erstwhile escorts. Soberly she admitted that Faisal's uncle might have grounds for doubting her suitability as a wife; but surely Faisal was capable of using his own judgment in these matters? He was not, after all, a child, and her anger at his uncle's casual dismissal of her burned afresh, bringing a sparkle to her eyes and a faint flush of colour to her cheeks.

Faisal had booked a table at one of the newer Mayfair clubs. The club had a gaming room, which was full of expensively jewelled women and their wealthy companions, but when they had eaten, it was to the dim privacy of the dance floor that Faisal led Felicia, taking her in his arms and holding her closely against him as they swayed to the strains of the latest poignant ballad.

It was stuffy on the dance floor, cigar smoke mingling with the rich perfumes of the women, and Felicia had left her jacket behind at their table. She wished Faisal would not hold her so tightly, nor so closely, but every time she tried to move slightly away, his grip tightened, a look in his eyes that warned her of the effect she was having upon him.

As they danced, she became uncomfortably aware of speculative eyes upon them as an Arab who had been at the gaming tables wandered across to watch the dancers.

She was just about to ask Faisal if he knew the onlooker, when he swore suddenly, releasing her, frowning, as he acknowledged the other man's presence.

'What's the matter?' Felicia protested, as he attempted to usher her off the floor.

'Do you know that man? He seems to be trying to attract your attention.'

'He is an acquaintance of my uncle's,' Faisal replied tersely. 'And he is bound to tell him that he saw us here together.'

'Does it matter?' Felicia protested in some bewilderment, unable to understand the reason for Faisal's annoyance.

'He is not a man of honourable reputation,' Faisal explained. 'I do not wish to introduce you to him, but if I do not, and he tells Raschid, Raschid will think I have not done so because I am ashamed of you. He will also think it not fitting that I bring you to such a place.'

'But that's ridiculous!' Felicia started to protest, falling silent as the Arab suddenly stepped out of the crowd in front of them.

'By the Prophet! Faisal al-Najar!' he exclaimed genially, but Felicia was aware of the speculation in his eyes, and flushed with embarrassment at the way they roved her body.

That Faisal was furious she could tell, and despite all the other man's attempts to draw him into conversation,

Faisal stubbornly insisted that they were on the point of
leaving and could not delay.

At first amused by his refusal to acknowledge *her* presence, Felicia's amusement gave way to annoyance when
he persisted in engaging Faisal in further conversation.
Listening rather half-heartedly to his description of events
which in no way included her, she learned that he had
been at the gaming tables when he saw them dancing and
that he had lost several thousand pounds. Even without
Faisal's remarks to colour her judgment Felicia knew
that she would not have liked him. He was shorter than
Faisal, built more on what she had always thought of as
'typically' Eastern lines, being rather squat with small,
narrow eyes which flicked lasciviously over her person to
return knowingly to Faisal's angry face.

'What's all this I hear about you going to New York?'
he exclaimed as they were on the point of leaving. 'Plenty
of obliging women there, my friend!'

He gave Faisal a look that made Felicia freeze with
resentment, longing to tell him that she was not Faisal's
mistress, but Faisal himself cut him short, exclaiming
angrily,

'I have no interest in the charms of other women. My
uncle may have told you that I hope to be married
shortly.'

Later, when they were on their way home, Felicia asked
Faisal if he thought it was wise to mention marriage,
especially when his uncle had not yet approved it, but
Faisal seemed to have lapsed into a brooding silence.

'By Allah, that he should dare to look at you so!' he
exclaimed violently, as he swung the car into the road
where she lived. His hands were clenched over the steering
wheel, and Felicia wondered if he was perhaps thinking
that had she been an Arab girl the confrontation would
never have been allowed to occur.

'Our last evening together, and it is quite spoiled!' In
that moment, with his handsome face marred by a scowl,

Felicia was hard put not to laugh. He reminded her so much of a small boy, thwarted in some desire.

'There will be other evenings,' she consoled him. 'And I'm coming to Heathrow with you tomorrow. I've never seen a Concorde before. I suppose you're travelling first-class?'

'Is there any other way?' he asked with a touch of hauteur that reminded her once again of the wide gulf that lay between them. He stopped the car, taking her in his arms, and kissing her with a fierce passion that previously he had always held in control. The violence of his emotions unnerved Felicia. She tried not to shrink under the pressure of his kiss, but he sensed her withdrawal, releasing her with a murmured apology.

'I forget how truly innocent you are. But soon we shall be man and wife, and then I shall teach you to respond to me, my cool white dove. I shall write to you, and you must write to me. You will soon be able to persuade my uncle to relent.'

He sounded so sure, so confident; but Felicia could not share his confidence. She was full of misgivings. Faisal's uncle would never accept her, and yet somehow she had to find a way of proving to him that she would make Faisal as good a wife as any Moslem girl.

Pride sparkled in her eyes. She would do it. She *would* find a way. She would show Faisal's uncle the stuff of which English girls were made!

CHAPTER TWO

Brave words! But she was feeling far from brave now, Felicia acknowledged as she stared out of the plane window and down on to the banked clouds below. Unbelievably, she had never flown before, Continental holidays being disapproved of by Uncle George, and outside her slender budget in any case.

The other passengers were obviously well seasoned travellers; businessmen with tired faces and bulging briefcases; Arabs in traditional white robes wearing headdresses held in place by the gold-wrapped frames she had learned from Faisal were called *igals*.

The Arab passengers were displaying a keen interest in the stewardesses, and watching the neatly uniformed girls going about their business. Felicia lost any envy she had ever had of their supposedly glamorous lives; the girls seemed to be little more than glorified waitresses! One of them had made a special point of putting her at her ease, showing her how to use the ear-phones that tuned into eight different channels of taped music, or permitted one to listen to the sound track of the in-flight film.

It was a long flight—six hours, although with the time difference Felicia knew that she would lose another three hours as Kuwait was three hours in front of Greenwich Mean Time, and many of the more seasoned travellers were apparently asleep. Felicia had started to watch the film, but the tight knot of tension that had been steadily taking possession of her insides from the moment the plane took off refused to let her relax, and after a very short time she abandoned the film, devoting her attention instead to her fellow travellers. Faisal had insisted that she travel first-class, and she was grateful for his insistence when she saw the cramped quarters of the economy cabin, full of what looked like entire Arab families, complete with crying babies and restless toddlers.

In the plane's hold was her shiny new luggage, all neatly labelled, and the small gifts she had purchased for Faisal's mother and sisters.

She had not bought anything for Faisal's uncle, quite deliberately so. They would not meet as friends and she was not going to give him the opportunity to hand her gift back to her with sneered accusations of bribery, or of trying to flatter him into acceptance of her.

And yet wasn't that exactly what Faisal wanted her to do? she asked herself uneasily; use her charm to try and sway his judgment? Her thoughts gave her no peace, jostling this way and that until her head ached with the effort of trying to reconcile her heart with her head. In the end she abandoned her efforts to put herself in the right frame of mind to meet Faisal's 'wicked uncle' and concentrated her thoughts instead on the other members of Faisal's family.

For his mother, who quite obviously worshipped him, she had bought perfume, and for his younger sister, soon to be married, a luxurious make-up kit with all the latest eye-shadows and lipsticks. His elder sister had been a little more difficult. Felicia knew that Nadia was married with a small child and that her husband was in charge of the Saudi Arabian branch of the family bank, so she had bought her an exquisite glass paperweight which had caught her eye in an expensive London store.

Indeed the paperweight was so beautiful that for an instant Felicia had been tempted to keep it for herself, but her present-buying had already stretched her slender budget to its limits and regretfully she admitted that she could not afford two such luxurious items; not when she had bought herself what amounted to a complete new wardrobe for this trip. Even now the extent of her spending spree dismayed her, but she wanted Faisal to be proud of her, so she had dipped quite deeply into the small nest egg she had been saving ever since she had started work.

When the skies opened out beneath them, and the businessmen began to ruffle their papers, Felicia guessed that they were nearing journey's end.

In the small washroom she inspected her make-up, hoping anxiously that the heat would not make her nose shine. Her skin was very fair and burned easily. She had deliberately used even less make-up than usual, not wanting to offend against Moslem tradition, and inspected her reflection anxiously in the mirror, hoping that she would not look too pale and washed out in comparison to the dusky Arabian beauties of Kuwait. Faisal had told her that in the Arab world, Kuwaiti women had the reputation of being the most beautiful, and she was dreading letting him down by comparing unfavourably with his countrywomen.

Strained green eyes stared nervously back at her, the length and thickness of her eyelashes startling against her pale skin. A faint flush of natural colour highlighted her high cheekbones, her mouth curving vulnerably beneath its covering of lip-gloss. She was wearing her hair loose, and it curled luxuriantly on to her shoulders, shimmering like raw silk whenever she moved. Should she wear it up in a discreet knot? she agonised, lifting it off her shoulders. It would look much tidier. Outside she heard the metallic request for seat belts to be fastened and realising that there was no time, she let it drop back on to her shoulders, running cold water over her wrists and dabbing on her favourite perfume, before hurrying back to her seat.

'Chanel Number Five—my favourite,' the stewardess commented with a smile, as Felicia sat down. 'Soon be down now.'

Felicia's stomach clenched as the big jet descended on to the runway. The engines screamed protestingly as the captain applied reverse thrust, then they were taxiing gently down the runway.

As she emerged from the aircraft, the heat and noisy bustle

of the airport almost threatened to overwhelm her, and then she was anxiously following the other disembarking passengers to have her visa and passport inspected.

The official who took her passport flashed her a warm, appreciative smile, as he glanced from her photograph to her face. There was a tiny scar high on her arm from the mandatory typhoid injection and tucked away in her handbag were the salt tablets Faisal had warned her that she would need as the temperature started to climb into the eighties and nineties.

Everyone apart from herself seemed to know exactly where they were going and what to do. An incomprehensible flood of Arabic washed all round her, punctuated here and there by heavily accented English from the taxi drivers and porters.

Felicia looked round in despair. Faisal had told her that she would be met at the airport, but by whom? Could one of these immaculately uniformed chauffeurs be waiting for her?

She was just debating the wisdom of making enquiries at the Tourist Information Desk, when a tall figure strode towards her, effortlessly parting the milling crowds.

'Miss Gordon?'

He was tall; taller than Faisal by several inches, and his voice held the certainty of a man who makes a statement rather than asks a question. She probably did stand out like a sore thumb, Felicia acknowledged wryly, but need he make her feel like an unwanted package he had come to collect?

She gave him a faltering smile, instantly quenched as she felt his cool scrutiny. Now, when it was too late, she wished that she had found time to put her hair up. It would have given her some badly needed sophistication. She darted her companion a surreptitious glance. Was he a relative of Faisal's, or just an employee sent to collect her?

'My luggage,' she murmured hesitantly, noticing the impatient manner in which he shot back the cuff of an

immaculate pale grey silk suit to glance at the heavy gold
Rolex watch strapped to his wrist. The gesture, so completely and arrogantly male, disturbed her, although she
could not have said why.

'Ali is collecting your luggage,' she was told. 'Come.'

He took her arm, propelling her through the crowd.
Even Felicia, inexperienced in these matters, was aware
of his aura of command. His clothes looked expensive, his
manner cool and decisive, and she decided that whoever
he was, he was obviously a man of some importance, used
to giving orders rather than taking them.

Dazzled by the colour and light, she hurried wearily
after him to a waiting Mercedes, humiliatingly forced to
drop behind him when his pace increased, for all the world
like some Moslem woman dutifully following her husband,
she thought wrathfully, as he paused to wait for her.

There was nothing welcoming in his manner. In fact
he seemed to derive considerable mocking amusement
from her hot and bothered state, and smiled, openly de-
risively, when two robed Arabs stopped to stare at her.

'Don't worry,' he told her sardonically, opening the car
door. 'The days are gone when an Arab was bowled over by
the pale beauty of Northern women. He has learned for
himself that they are not as chaste as their appearance
leads him to believe!'

In the sunshine his hair had the blue-black gleam of a
raven's wing, thick, and long enough to cover the collar
of his suit. He wasn't wearing sunglasses, and Felicia was
surprised to see that his eyes were grey and not brown, a
cold, hard grey like the North Sea in winter. She shivered
suddenly, and a chill ran over her despite the heat.

When she hesitated by the car he raised his eyebrows in
silent mockery.

'A plane leaves for England in three hours, if you have
changed your mind,' he told her.

Changed her mind? Felicia shot him a suspicious
glance. Was that what he had been expecting? Was that
why he had been so offhand with her? Obviously Faisal's

uncle had confided in him, and her soft lips tightened at the thought of the two of them discussing her disparagingly. No doubt for all his outward Westernised appearance this man was as much a traditionalist as Faisal's uncle. He had looked her over and found her wanting. She tilted her chin and looked up at him bravely, quelling her fear. Already the sun was dropping over the horizon with a speed that surprised her, used as she was to the more leisurely sunsets of more northerly climes.

'I am not going back,' she told him firmly.

In the silence that prickled between them she could almost feel his antagonism and then he was holding open the car door, his expression unfathomable.

'Please get in, Miss Gordon,' he requested curtly. 'It is an hour's drive to the villa.'

Did he have to make her feel like a stupid child? she asked herself crossly, as she got into the Mercedes. After all, despite his air of authority he could scarcely be much more than thirty-two or three—a little more than ten years older than she was herself.

The chauffeur—who she gussed must be 'Ali'—appeared with her luggage, which was stowed away in the trunk, and then they were driving out of the airport and down a wide tarmac road in the direction of Kuwait itself.

Felicia stole a glance at her companion's impassive face. He must know how strange and nervous she felt, and yet he made no attempt to put her at her ease—very well, she decided mutinously, *she* was not going to be the one to end the smothering silence. He moved slightly, thick black lashes veiling his eyes as he turned his head suddenly to look at her. Colour flooded her cheeks. Now he would think she had been staring at him! Hateful man!

'No doubt Faisal has prepared you for the kind of life we live here in Kuwait,' he drawled coolly in perfect accentless English, which Felicia suspected was the product of an exclusive public school.

'He has spoken to me of his family, yes,' she replied equally disdainfully. She paused deliberately, then added, as though it were an afterthought, 'And of his uncle, of course. You know him?'

'To judge from the exceedingly challenging note in your voice, you have already come to your own conclusions,' her companion replied very dryly. 'But I shall answer your question anyway. Yes, I know him.'

'And you know that he does not approve of our engagement as well, I suppose?' Felicia said bitterly.

'Engagement?'

Did she imagine the faint hardening of those cruel lips as they looked down at her ringless hand?

'Faisal wanted us to be engaged,' she flashed back, thoroughly enraged, 'but I prefer to wait until we can have the sanction of his family.'

'How very wise!' he mocked sardonically. 'But then of course any marriage without Raschid's approval would result in a discontinuation of Faisal's extremely generous allowance, as I am sure you already know.'

His words shocked Felicia into momentary silence, and then colour stormed her pale face as she contemplated their significance. Her fingers clenched into small, impotent fists. How dared he insinuate that she had deliberately and calculatedly persuaded Faisal to wait because she was motivated by greed? If Faisal's uncle thought like this man she would have no hope of persuading him to accept her. The thought made her reckless.

'I would have married Faisal without his uncle's sanction,' she stormed, 'but he didn't want to cause a rift in his family. His money means nothing to me. It's him that I love!'

'And that is why he has sent you to persuade Raschid? You with your red-gold hair and sea-green eyes? Did he tell you that you bear an unmistakable resemblance to Raschid's grandmother?'

Felicia's colour betrayed her, and he surveyed her in silent contempt, his eyes cold.

'You have come on a fool's errand, Miss Gordon. Faisal knows that Raschid will not give his consent to any betrothal. Indeed I suspect this is merely another of his attempts to persuade Raschid to release to him the control of his inheritance. How much is he paying you to come here and. . . .'

'It's not like that!' Felicia stormed. 'I love Faisal and he loves me. . . .'

'How very touching!' he mocked, ignoring her distress. 'But Raschid will never give his consent.'

His arrogance infuriated her.

'How do you know?' she demanded incautiously. 'Who are you to speak for him?'

'Who am I?' he repeated softly, his eyes narrowed and watching. 'Why, Miss Gordon, I thought you must have guessed. I *am* Faisal's uncle, Sheikh Raschid al Hamid Al Sabah.' Mocking irony informed the words, and Felicia was glad of the encroaching dusk to mask her confusion. She suppose she ought to have guessed, she thought tiredly, but somehow she had it firmly fixed in her mind that Raschid would be a much older man. He had deliberately deceived her, she thought angrily, aware of the merciless scrutiny of cold grey eyes that told her how much he was enjoying her embarrassment.

You can't be Raschid, she wanted to protest. She had expected a man of middle age, with a greying beard and the traditional flowing white robes; this man with his expensive European clothes and elegantly groomed appearance bore no resemblance at all to the Raschid of her imaginings.

He had tricked her into a trap, and she had foolishly helped him, but there was one point at least that she could make clear.

'I *do* love Faisal,' she told him shakily. 'And I loved him before I knew he was your nephew.'

Green eyes clashed with grey, but it was Felicia's that dropped first.

'And what, I wonder, is that supposed to mean?'

At his side Felicia fumed silently. He had already trapped her into enough indiscretion; she was not going to compound her folly by admitting that she suspected he believed her interest in Faisal stemmed from avarice.

They were driving through the heart of the city and she roused herself sufficiently to stare interestedly out of the car window, ignoring the silent disparagement of the man at her side. Faisal had told her that his family lived on the coast between Kuwait and the town of Al Jahrah, although apparently his uncle had a villa at the oasis which had been the original home of their tribe.

'This is Arabian Gulf Street,' Raschid informed her dryly. 'It runs along the coast. If you look carefully you will see the Sief Palace.'

Mutinously Felicia ignored him, staring resolutely through the window. As the car swept down the road a shattering wail broke the silence, jerking her upright to stare wide-eyed out of the car.

'The muezzin,' her companion said sardonically. 'This is the hour of sunset when the faithful must face Mecca and pray, but if you expect to see them do so in the streets as they once did, you will be disappointed, Miss Gordon. Nowadays our lives are ruled by more mundane needs than prayer.'

'But you're a Christian,' Felicia began impulsively, remembering what Faisal had told her, and falling silent when she saw the anger tightening his face.

'By baptism, yes,' he agreed curtly. 'But make no mistake, I live my life according to the laws of my family, laws which Faisal's wife will have to obey as implicitly as he does himself. Make no mistake, Miss Gordon, my English blood will not incline me to look favourably upon you, no matter what Faisal might have told you.'

Felicia snatched a look at the forbidding line of his mouth, and knew that he meant what he said. Despair filled her. She had promised Faisal that she would do her best to impress his uncle, and yet already she had aroused his anger and, worse, his contempt. Crossly she bit her lip, fuming in silence until they were clear of the town, the powerful car carrying them swiftly through the sub-urbs, where houses of all shapes and designs jostled one another, the scent of lime trees heavy on the evening air, when Raschid pressed the button to wind down his window and throw out the stub of the thin cigar he had been smoking.

'Still sulking?' he drawled when Felicia remained silent. 'And yet I am sure Faisal impressed upon you the im-portance of gaining my goodwill.'

'Which we both know will never be forthcoming,' Felicia shot back unwisely. 'I know why you suggested this visit. You wanted to part us, to prove to Faisal that I will not make him a good wife, to make him have second thoughts. . . .' To her horror her voice wavered and weak tears blurred her vision. 'Well, you won't succeed!' she stormed at him. 'We love each other, and I would still love him even if he were a beggar!'

Her companion's mouth twisted sardonically.

'Woman's eternal cry when she knows there is little chance of it coming to pass. Faisal could no more live in poverty than you could yourself.' He looked at the expensive linen suit she had bought for travelling, his eyes mocking. 'Look at yourself, Miss Gordon. From the top of your undeniably lovely head to the tips of your feet, you evidence expensive grooming. Do you honestly expect me to believe that you would live in poverty with my nephew—a boy who has never wanted for anything in his life?'

But I have wanted, Felicia wanted to throw at him. And I've wanted the most important thing of all—love! But she knew better than to expect the man seated oppo-site her to understand her deep-seated need for that. Money was all he understood, she thought bitterly. Money and power.

'I know what you're trying to do,' she said eventually, 'but you won't succeed. You're a cruel, hard man, Sheikh, and I know you for my enemy!'

In the darkness she saw the white flash of his smile.

'Enemies?' His voice was like velvet. 'Is that what you think? In our country there is no enmity between man and woman.'

'There is between the hawk and the dove, though,' Felicia retorted, 'and that's what you are—a cruel predator, determined to destroy our love.'

'And you are the dove?'

He was sneering openly, his eyes contemptuous as they rested on her slender form beneath its linen covering. 'Vulture would be a more appropriate description, don't you agree?'

There was nothing to be gained by arguing with him, Felicia thought, blinking away weak tears. The uncle of her imaginings had been bad enough, but the reality was far worse. She, who had never hated anyone in her life, disliked him so acutely that the emotion was almost tangible, filling the silence between them with crackling hostility as the car swept past the oil tank farm, the glare from the oilfields illuminating the distant horizon, a sombre reminder that she changed her world for Faisal's.

They were travelling parallel to the coast, the sky like a dark blue velvet cloak sewn with diamonds. If only Faisal was with her, Felicia thought unhappily. At this moment she needed the warm protection of his love as she had never needed it before.

'Don't bother to assume an air of mock modesty for my benefit, Miss Gordon,' Raschid advised her coldly. 'I have already learned how you comport yourself, from a friend who observed your antics on the dance floor with my nephew.'

The words were icy with a disdain that drove the colour from Felicia's face. Her hands gripped together in her lap to stop them from trembling.

'Apparently Faisal all but stripped you where you stood,' the bored voice continued sardonically, 'and you apparently made no protest at all. Do you honestly believe that is the sort of behaviour a Moslem tolerates in a wife, or is it that having already granted Faisal the privileges of a husband, you feel confident enough to behave exactly as you wish?'

Felicia all but choked in her fury. Hot colour stained her cheeks. How dared he imply. . . . 'Your friend!' she managed to grit at him. 'I suppose you mean that horrid man who looked at me as though I were a piece of merchandise he was contemplating buying?'

'Perhaps he was,' came the uncaring retort. 'It is a long time since I was last in London, but my friends are amused by the low price your women put upon themselves. The British were once greatly respected, but who can respect a race that allows its women to sell themselves for so little?'

She was going to be sick, Felicia thought wretchedly. She could not listen to any more of this.

'Faisal and I were *dancing*—nothing more.'

'Do you always *dance* so close to your partner that you could be making love?' was the biting response.

Felicia suppressed an urge to demand him to stop the car so that she could get out. He was deliberately and relentlessly destroying the fabric of her dreams, but she could not let him see it.

'It was nothing like that,' she told Raschid coolly. 'Faisal respects me.'

Just for a second she thought she saw shock mingled with anger, in his eyes, and then he had himself under control.

'Does he indeed?' he drawled speculatively. 'Then he is even more of a fool that I had imagined.'

The dulcet words held a subtle threat. She had handed him a weapon, Felicia acknowledged unhappily, and one that he would not hesitate to use against her if he ever got the opportunity.

'If you were so convinced of my moral laxness, why did you invite me here?' she challenged. 'Aren't you afraid that I might contaminate Faisal's sister with my wanton behaviour?'

Raschid ignored her wild outburst, studying one elegant gold cufflink with apparent absorption for so long that she almost wanted to scream.

'I have sufficient faith in my niece to know she would not be influenced by you,' he announced at last. 'And as to my reasons for asking you here. . . . You are an intelligent woman, Miss Gordon, what do you think?'

'I don't think you wanted me here at all,' Felicia accused slowly. 'You never really wanted to get to know me, did you?'

'Most astute,' Raschid acknowledged dryly. 'But now that you are here, let me make one thing quite clear. You are here strictly on sufferance. My sister knows only that you are a friend of Faisal's—nothing more, and that is all she will know . . .'

'Until I can prove that I'm fit to marry her son,' Felicia interrupted angrily. 'Well, I don't care what you think of me, but if it makes Faisal happy I'm quite willing to go through this farce of trying to get your approval. After all, in three years' time he'll be free to marry without it in any case.'

His expression warned her that she had angered him deeply. His voice harsh, he said coldly, 'You are more determined than I realised, but then with good cause. After all, you do not have much to look forward to in England, do you? A very run-of-the-mill job; an aunt in the North of England who may or may not leave her home to you, and very little else. . . .'

'Must you reduce everything to terms of money?' Felicia protested bitterly. 'If I'd merely wanted financial security I could have married before now.'

'But instead you chose to wait until a more attractive proposition presented itself to you,' the hateful voice drawled smoothly. 'How wise of you!'

Wearily Felicia sank back into the leather seat. What was the use of trying to convince him? She was wasting her time. He was determined to believe the worst of her. For a moment she contemplated demanding that he turn the car round and take her back to the airport, but to do so would be to acknowledge him the victor, and that was something she would never do. After all, she knew that she was none of the things he believed, and surely, in time, by just being herself, she would prove to him beyond any shadow of a doubt just how lacking his judgment had been.

This thought was enough to quell her desire to return home. Faisal loved her, and this was the raft to which she would cling throughout the stormy seas of Raschid's displeasure.

Some hidden well of courage she had not hitherto plumbed enabled her to face Raschid with a composure to match his own, her voice controlled as she said calmly:

'If you have so little faith in Faisal's ability to choose a wife for himself, I'm surprised that you didn't do it for him—an arranged marriage with the bride carefully selected to match up to his uncle's very exacting standards.'

She had meant the words as a taunt, but something in Raschid's face warned her that all unsuspectingly she had stumbled upon the truth. Pressing a hand to her aching temple, she whispered,

'Was there a girl? No, I don't believe it. Faisal would never. . . .'

'You'd be surprised what folly young men will perpetrate in the name of love, Miss Gordon.' Raschid's hard voice cut through her protests. 'But in this case there was no actual betrothal. I did not consider Faisal mature enough to take on the responsibilities of a wife. You are not the first young woman with whom he has considered himself "in love", but you are certainly the first with whom he has actually contemplated marriage. The others were content with a more tenuous relationship.'

Felicia refused to believe it. And yet hadn't she already guessed that Faisal was nowhere near as inexperienced as she was herself? At the time she had smothered the thought, but now it was resurrected, and she was forced to acknowledge that there were parts of Faisal's life of which he had told her nothing. But what really hurt was that Raschid should so casually condemn her to the ranks of those girls with whom Faisal had enjoyed a brief affair. Surely his own knowledge of his nephew told him that Faisal would never have contemplated marriage unless he was sure of his feelings?

'Faisal is young, and impetuous,' Raschid drawled, as though he had read her mind, 'and the two do not make for good judgment. You have known one another a matter of weeks only, what basis is that for a lifetime together!'

A moment was all it took to fall in love, Felicia wanted to protest, but dismay kept her silent. She was seeing a side to Faisal that she had not known existed. In her eyes he was a protective, although sometimes, admittedly, impatient man. In Raschid's he was an impulsive boy, falling in and out of love on the whim of the moment. Which of them was right? She gave herself a mental shake. She was, of course. How could she doubt it?

The car swerved off the main road and at her side she felt Raschid move slightly to adjust to the slight sway of the car.

'Not much farther now,' he told her coolly. 'Faisal's mother and sister have delayed the evening meal to coincide with your arrival. I hope you like traditional Kuwaiti food, Miss Gordon?'

As he stretched lithely, she wondered at the glint of humour in his eyes. Was his amusement at her expense? If so he would be disappointed. Faisal had already assured her that while his mother preferred to stick to the old ways, his sisters had insisted that they eat in the European fashion instead of seated cross-legged on the floor, and that she need have no fears about being offered some choice morsel such as sheep's eyes, or something equally unpalatable. In fact he had once taken her to a small restaurant in London where they had eaten delicious saffron rice and kebabs, followed by almond pastry and small cups of coffee, and she had thoroughly enjoyed it.

She was well and truly caught between the devil and

the deep, Felicia acknowledged as the powerful car purred along. On the one hand, if she flouted Raschid and informed Faisal's mother of their engagement, she would incur his immediate displeasure, and yet if she said nothing he would take her acquiescence as a sign that she was deliberately trying to court his approval. If only Faisal were not dependent upon his goodwill—but she knew it was useless to dwell on this. Naturally Faisal would want to take his rightful place in the family business, which meant that they would probably not be able to marry until he was twenty-five—aeons away to someone with such a volatile nature as Raschid claimed Faisal possessed. There was no doubt at all in her own mind that Raschid hoped that during their enforced separation Faisal would find himself someone else, and helpless with impotent anger, she stared bleakly out into the darkness, wishing she had never been foolish enough to accept Raschid's invitation.

They were travelling through empty countryside, with the sea on one side of them, and what Felicia took to be the open desert on the other. Even though Faisal had prepared her for Kuwait's modern outlook, her first glimpse of the family villa still caught her off guard. She did not know quite what she had expected, but it was not this large, two-storey building, with its painted shutters and white walls, vaguely reminiscent of the Moorish houses of Andalucia; not at least until she remembered the origins of those same Moors.

Without checking the Mercedes slid through an arched gateway and across a flagged courtyard, decorated with urns of tumbling flowers. Lights shone from several windows illuminating the courtyard and others beyond it, where she could just see the outline of trees, and hear the musical tinkle of fountains.

Raschid opened the car door for her, and she drew in a shaky breath of fresh air spiced with unfamiliar scents.

'This way, Miss Gordon.'

It was a command, and she responded unthinkingly,

wondering at his ability to cloak his dislike of her in such formal politeness.

Her earlier attack of nerves was nothing to what she was experiencing now. What was she going to do if the rest of Faisal's family were as hostile towards her as his uncle? She tried not to dwell on the thought as the wooden door was flung open and she stood in a rectangle of light.

'Fatima, this is Miss Gordon,' Raschid said to the small, plump woman who stood there. 'Miss Gordon—my sister, Faisal's mother.'

Felicia's sharp ears caught the warning beneath the coolly drawled words, as she extended her hand slowly to the woman watching her.

It was taken between two soft, beringed hands, while Faisal's mother beamed at her, chattering incomprehensibly to the tall man at her side.

'In English, Fatima,' Raschid told her. 'Miss Gordon does not have any Arabic.'

Another black mark against her, Felicia reflected bitterly, but Raschid was wrong. She did know how to say 'good evening', thanks to Faisal, although it was difficult to get her tongue round the unfamiliar Arabic words.

'*Massa'a al-Khayr*,' Faisal's mother responded delightedly, darting a mischievous look at her brother.

'There you are, Raschid!' she exclaimed in heavily accented English. 'She does speak Arabic.'

'Only a few phrases,' Felicia protested apologetically. 'And Faisal laughs at my pronunciation.'

'Poor Miss Gordon!' another female voice chimed in prettily. 'Let her get into the house before you start cross-questioning her about Faisal, Mother.'

'Zahra, what will Miss Gordon think of you?' her mother chided. 'Young people today have no manners.' She turned to Felicia. 'Please ignore this foolish child. She teases me because I am anxious about Faisal, but when she has a son of her own, then she will feel differently . . .'

So this was Faisal's younger sister, Zahra. Felicia

studied her covertly. She was small, plump like her
mother, with sparkling dark eyes, and a warm smile that
held none of Raschid's cold reserve. Faisal had neglected
to tell her how pretty his sister was, Felicia reflected,
relieved to see that Zahra at least seemed to harbour no
dislike for her.

'You will sleep in the room next to mine,' Zahra explained as she led her upstairs. 'Mother would stick to the
old ways of keeping to the women's quarters, if she could,
but although we use our own sitting room whenever Faisal
or Uncle Raschid entertain business colleagues, Raschid
does not believe in women being strictly segregated.' She
pulled a wry face. 'Mother is dreadfully old-fashioned.
She hated it when I first started at university, but Uncle
Raschid was insistent, thank goodness. I hope you are
hungry? Mother has had a feast prepared for you, although I warned her that you might not be hungry,
having travelled so far.'

Mentally blessing Zahra for her tactful warning of what to
expect, Felicia shook her head. In point of fact she felt
exhausted and longed only for a hot bath and a comfortable
bed, but it would be bad manners to show anything less than
immense pleasure in her hostess's preparations—she knew
enough about Arab protocol to be aware of that!

'Faisal has written to me about you,' Zahra confided,
eyeing Felicia speculatively. 'You are to become betrothed . . .'

'Perhaps,' Felicia tempered, remembering Raschid's
warning. 'Provided your uncle approves of me.'

Her room overlooked the gardens and was quite
Western in concept, with a comfortable single bed and
modern fitted bedroom furniture along one wall, with
hanging space for far more clothes than Felicia had
brought. There was a bathroom off it, tiled in deep pink
to match the sanitary fittings which all boasted gold taps
and wastes, and were quite obviously all of the very most
luxurious quality.

'I hope you weren't expecting sunken baths with marble

pillars,' Zahra giggled. 'Uncle Raschid swore you would expect us to live like something out of the Thousand and One Nights.'

'Well, I did wonder how you managed those flimsy trousers and curly-toed shoes,' Felicia agreed lightly, earning an approving grin from Zahra.

'I knew that you would have a sense of humour, despite what Uncle Raschid said!'

And what exactly had that been? Felicia wondered grimly. Plainly Zahra knew about their plans, although she suspected that Raschid had also warned the younger girl not to mention them to her mother.

'If you *do* have a hankering to see the old Kuwait, you must ask Uncle Raschid to take you to his villa at the oasis,' Zahra surprised her by saying. 'It was built by his grandfather, although he rarely used it. He preferred to travel with his people and live in their black tents. He built it for his English wife. Leave your unpacking,' she instructed, changing the subject. 'One of the maids will do that for you. Are you ready to eat?'

Guessing that she had already delayed the family meal long beyond its normal hour, Felicia assured her that she was quite ready.

As they went downstairs, Zahra explained to her that the house was built around the enclosed gardens she had noticed on her arrival, and that it comprised the traditional women's quarters, with two separate wings; one of which was used by Raschid and the other being set aside for Faisal's use when he was at home.

'Not that Raschid sticks rigidly to his quarters,' Zahra explained. 'He normally eats with us unless business prevents him. In my father's time the women never ate with the men, but things are different now, and Uncle Raschid encouraged both Nadia and myself to take advantage of a modern education.'

'How kind of him,' Felicia murmured sarcastically. She was surprised to discover that Zahra evidently held her uncle in great affection, but wished she had not given vent to her own feelings for him when Zahra paused to eye her enquiringly.

'Don't you like Raschid?'

'I haven't known him long enough to form an opinion,' Felicia countered diplomatically, but Zahra was not deceived, and chuckled, explaining,

'When we heard you were coming, I think Mother was frightened that you would fall in love with him. All my friends think he's wonderful, and when he was at university in England he had many girl-friends.'

I'll bet he did, Felicia thought sourly, and she could just imagine his lordly reaction to them.

'He is very good-looking, isn't he?' Zahra murmured judiciously. 'Much more so than Faisal.'

'But not as gentle or kind,' Felicia responded before she could stop herself.

Zahra's brown eyes twinkled with amusement.

'Zut! Kindness! Is that what you look for in a man? I think Uncle Raschid is wrong when he says you are experienced in the ways of men, otherwise you would know that kindness is not necessary between a man and a woman, where there is love.'

She said it so seriously that Felicia could not contradict her, although her own love-starved childhood had taught her that kindness was a precious virtue. Perhaps the harshness of their desert climate bred the need for it out of these people, she reflected. To her amusement Zahra was dressed in jeans and a thin T-shirt, her long hair caught back off her face with a ribbon, and as they entered what was obviously the family dining room, Felicia noticed the younger girl's mother frowning rather despairingly as her eyes alighted on her daughter.

'Raschid, you must speak to this child,' she protested. 'Look at her!'

'Mother, everyone at the university wears jeans,' Zahra laughed, 'and Uncle Raschid will not forbid me, because he wears them himself,' she said triumphantly. 'I have seen him.'

Faisal's mother looked at her brother, as though seeking confirmation, and although his mouth twitched a little he betrayed no embarrassment.

'Maybe so,' he allowed, 'but not at the dinner table. Tonight we shall excuse you, but in future, unless you come to dinner properly dressed you will eat alone in the women's quarters.'

Zahra pulled a face, but subsided a little, obviously accepting that Raschid would put his threat into practice if she defied him.

'Come, we must eat. Miss Gordon. . . .'

'Oh, call her Felicia, Mother,' Zahra cried impetuously. 'And she must call you Umm Faisal.'

Felicia was about to demur, conscious of Raschid's cool scrutiny, and her own tenuous position in the family, when Faisal's mother looked anxiously at her, and said something in Arabic to her brother.

'My sister begs you not to take offence at Zahra's impetuosity, Miss Gordon,' he said sardonically. 'She had intended to ask you herself to do her the favour of calling her "Umm Faisal", but Zahra has forestalled her. She also reminds me that as I am head of our family it is my duty to welcome you to our home, and beg you to treat our humble dwelling as your own for as long as it pleases you to remain with us.'

While there was no doubting the sincerity of Faisal's mother's welcome, Felicia stiffened, knowing that Raschid did not mean a word of what he was saying. His expression told her that much. However, before she could say anything, Zahra caused a minor disturbance by remarking teasingly.

'Miss Gordon! You cannot call her that, Uncle Raschid, not when she is to . . . not when she is such a close friend of Faisal's,' she amended hurriedly. 'You must call her Felicia—mustn't he?'

She turned to Felicia for corroboration, unaware of the cold antipathy in her uncle's eyes as they skimmed the slender figure of the girl standing in the shadows.

Personally she did not care what Raschid called her, although she was sure he had adopted the formal 'Miss Gordon' to remind her that he wanted to keep her at a distance. Fortunately no one else seemed to be aware of the antagonism pulsating between them, and Felicia was invited to sit down and help herself to the food set before them. Despite the variety of dishes pressed upon her, she could barely touch a morsel. She did her best, glad of Zahra's distracting chatter, and answering her many questions as best she could. A curious dreamlike state seemed to have engulfed her, and it was all she could do to keep her eyes open. Her heart felt weighted with despair, and nausea churned her stomach—a legacy of her long flight, and the confrontation with Raschid, she acknowledged wearily.

Once or twice during the long meal she suffered the disturbing sensation of the room blurring and fading, although on each occasion she managed to jerk herself back to awareness.

'Are you feeling all right, Felicia?' Zahra asked in some concern, observing the other girl's increasing pallor, but Felicia shook her head, not wishing to draw the attention of cold grey eyes to her predicament.

Later she was to regret this foolish pride, but as she struggled to swallow another mouthful of almond pastry and drink a cup of coffee she was concentrating all her energy on merely quelling her growing nausea, from one moment to the next.

At long last the ordeal was over. Shakily Felicia got to her feet, swaying slightly as faintness swept her, and from a distance she heard Zahra cry anxiously,

'Quick, she's falling!'

And then there was nothing but the blessed peace of enveloping darkness and the strength of arms that gripped her, halting the upward rush of the beautiful crimson Persian carpet she had previously been admiring.

CHAPTER THREE

'WILL she be all right?'

The anxious question hovered somewhere on the outer periphery of her subconscious, registering in a dim and distant fashion even while its import eluded her. The voice was familiar, though, and Felicia struggled to recognise it. Mercifully, someone else took on the responsibility of replying, a male voice, deep, crisp, with faintly indolent overtones; a voice that sent small feather tendrils of fear curling insidiously down her spine, so that she was tempted to curl up into a small ball and hide away from it.

'Don't worry, Zahra. It's a combination of exhaustion and temperature change, I suspect, coupled with too much rich food on an empty stomach.—Now you know why your mother forbids you to go on these ridiculous slimming diets.'

'Felicia doesn't need to slim,' Zahra objected. 'She looks so pale, Raschid. Don't you think we ought to send for a doctor?'

Raschid! Now she remembered! Felicia opened her eyes, wincing in the electric light, forcing away the darkness that reached out for her and struggling to sit up. She was in her bedroom—she recognised that much at least—and Umm Faisal was hovering anxiously in the doorway, while Zahra and Raschid stood by her bed.

'I don't need a doctor,' she croaked, disconcerted when all three pairs of eyes focused at once upon her.

'You've come round!' Zahra exclaimed thankfully. 'We were so worried about you. What could we have told Faisal if you had fallen ill?'

'I'm sure Faisal would have agreed with me that Miss Gordon should have told us she was feeling unwell,'

Raschid interrupted unsympathetically. 'Zahra, find one of the maids and get some fresh fruit juice for our patient. After her long flight she is probably somewhat dehydrated, and perhaps a sleeping pill will help Miss Gordon to get a good night's sleep, Fatima?'

'Didn't anyone warn you that jet travel can be extremely dehydrating?' Raschid asked her severely as his sister and niece hurried to do his bidding. Felicia closed her eyes, turning her face to the wall, dismayed to hear him drawl mockingly,

'Still hating me, Miss Gordon? How wise of you not to try to deny it. Your eyes smoulder in a most disconcerting fashion when you are angry, but you had best not let my sister see them. She comes from a generation that believes implicitly in the absolute supremacy of the male.'

'Then you must be a throwback!' Felicia muttered unwisely under her breath, shocked when, without warning, Raschid's fingers grasped her chin, forcing her face round so that she was obliged to endure his cool scrutiny.

'What can have happened to all your good intentions?' he mocked unkindly. 'Were we not agreed that for Faisal's sake you must seek my approval, or are you perhaps foolish enough to believe that this *is* the way to do so? Allow me to disillusion you. Do not continue this foolish and pointless defiance. I am not renowned for my patience, Miss Gordon, but neither am I the monster of your imaginings. Faisal is an extremely wealthy and spoilt young man. I am his guardian—for my sins—and although I cannot stop him marrying where he chooses, I do have the means to delay that marriage if I am not convinced that it is right for him. If you really seek his happiness you must see the sense of what I am saying.'

'Is it so difficult for you to accept that his happiness lies with me?' Felicia countered shakily, determined to withstand the fierce onslaught of his gaze. 'You talk to me of sense and reason, and yet you condemned me without knowing the first thing about me. Whether you admit it or not you don't want Faisal to marry me. And yet why?

By what right do you take it upon yourself to choose for
him? You know nothing about me. How can you say that
we won't be happy?'

'Zut! Either you are an imbecile or a stubborn fool,
Miss Gordon. Faisal is a Moslem—an Arab, with all that
the word encompasses. You are British. Even today the
two worlds lie far apart. Marriage to Faisal would make
you his possession, every bit as much as his car or his
home.'

'Perhaps I *want* to be,' Felicia retorted, refusing to be
quelled.

Raschid's expression was sardonic. 'You may want him
to possess your body, Miss Gordon,' he stated baldly, 'but,
as you will discover if you do marry Faisal, he will own
you body *and* soul.'

'I thought women weren't supposed to have souls,'
Felicia commented rather unwisely. 'I thought they were
just men's playthings; bearers of children. You won't
frighten me by telling me these things. If you honestly
believe a Moslem woman to be an inferior being, why do
you let Zahra attend university?'

'We are not talking of my beliefs, Miss Gordon,' he
reminded her coolly, 'but those of my nephew. Do not
deceive yourself. For all his outward Westernised views,
Faisal is every bit as conservative as his father, and his
father before him. He may not expect you to go into
purdah or veil yourself, but he will not countenance a loss
of face because you, his wife—his possession—refuse to
acknowledge his superiority.'

His ears, sharper than hers, caught the sound of feet on
the stairs, and he frowned warningly. A hectic flush
stained Felicia's previously pale face. She was so angry
that she trembled beneath his suave gaze.

'This is neither the time nor the place to discuss these
matters,' Raschid told her. 'We shall talk again when you
are rested, but I warn you now that nothing you have
said so far has done anything to convince me that you
could make Faisal happy. Marriage is a serious business,

Miss Gordon, not to be undertaken on a mere whim.'

'How would you know?' Felicia muttered bitterly, as Zahra bustled in. 'You've never been married, have you?'

He turned on his heel, ignoring her taunt, and when he had gone Zahra cast a nervous glance at the closed door.

'Felicia, you have been quarrelling with Raschid, haven't you?' she whispered.

'I think you can guess why. He doesn't want me to marry Faisal,' Felicia told her bleakly, driven by the need to confide in someone.

'I know,' Zahra admitted. 'He has spoken of this to me. You must not get upset, Felicia, it is just that Faisal. . . .' she coloured, patently embarrassed. 'Well, you are not the first girl he has believed himself in love with, and Uncle Raschid is merely anxious to protect my mother. She does not understand these things. To her a betrothal is as sacred as a marriage, and that is why Uncle Raschid will not allow you to become engaged until he is sure that your marriage will be a happy one.'

In other circumstances Felicia might have seen the wisdom behind these words, but Raschid's implied criticism of Faisal fuelled her anger, causing Zahra to eye her with growing concern as indignant colour burned her cheeks.

'You must have patience,' Zahra soothed. 'Raschid will come round in time, I am sure of it. You must have *siyasa.*'

'*Siyasa?* What is that?' Felicia enquired, intrigued in spite of herself.

Zahra laughed. 'It is what in England you would call tact, but more! It is the art of getting what you want without forcing the other man to lose face.'

'It is obvious that your uncle does not think me deserving of *siyasa,*' Felicia complained. 'I honestly believe he wants to humiliate me!'

Zahra made a shocked, tutting sound.

'Never would he be so impolite to a guest,' she averred firmly. 'He is merely anxious for my mother. He wishes to protect her, that is all. Marriage is a big step. . . .'

'So your uncle was telling me,' Felicia agreed wryly. 'He seems to be quite an expert on the subject, although he isn't married himself.'

'That is because his betrothed died,' Zahra explained in a low voice. 'It used to be the custom for a girl to be engaged to her first cousin, and this practice was adopted by Raschid's father, so that Raschid is my mother's brother, but he was also my father's cousin.'

It was all rather difficult for Felicia to assimilate, with an aching head, but she did her best.

'Raschid is, of course, my mother's stepbrother,' Zahra continued. 'He was the child of my grandfather's second wife. That is why he is of your religion and we are not. Faisal will have told you something of this?'

'He told me that your uncle's grandmother was an English girl—a Christian,' Felicia admitted, curious, despite her averred dislike of Faisal's uncle.

'Yes, that is so,' Zahra agreed. 'Raschid's grandparents met in the desert, when he rescued her from a sandstorm. They fell deeply in love and since Raschid's grandfather was the head of his family he was free to marry whomever he chose. It was for her that he built the house at the oasis, for despite their love sometimes she yearned for her old life amongst her own people. Raschid's mother was their only child, and she was the second wife of my grandfather. That is how Raschid comes to be Christian. It is a romantic story, is it not?'

Felicia allowed that it was.

'I do not think Raschid will marry now,' Zahra mused. 'I think he enjoys his single state too much.' She dimpled a smile at Felicia. 'Mother is constantly suggesting this girl or that, for his approval, but he always has an excuse.'

'Another example of *siyasa*!' Felicia commented dryly, wincing when Zahra clapped her hands and laughed.

'I am going to enjoy having you staying with us, Felicia. Poor Uncle Raschid! He will not be able to stand out against you for long, especially when Faisal comes home. Mother has always spoiled him dreadfully, and I don't think she would object if he took *four* English wives!'

Umm Faisal might not, Felicia thought tiredly, but she certainly would. She closed her eyes, trying to relax and ease the tension from her muscles, but Raschid's darkly sardonic features would keep transposing themselves between her aching head and the peace she sought.

In the end she welcomed Umm Faisal's entrance, to bear her chattering daughter away and leave her guest a glass of chilled fruit juice and the promised sleeping tablet.

It was the unfamiliar figure of the maid tiptoeing past the window that eventually woke Felicia. She opened her eyes, disorientated, and wondering where she was, and then the events of the previous day came flooding back. Of course! She was in Kuwait faced with the seemingly impossible mission of trying to persuade Sheikh Raschid to accept her into his family.

The maid threw back the curtains with a shy smile, but in response to Felicia's questions, she only shook her head and left the room, reappearing several minutes later with Umm Faisal.

'So! You are feeling better?' the older woman exclaimed in her slow English, giving her guest a beaming smile. 'That is good. Zahra has gone to the university, but she left a message to say that she will meet you in Kuwait later in the day. Ali will take you in the car and wait for you.'

'Zahra has left?' Felicia sat up and stared disbelievingly at her watch. How on earth could it be eleven in the morning? When she broke into an appalled apology Umm Faisal shook her head, plainly undisturbed.

'It is the pill,' she assured Felicia, 'and you will feel better for the long sleep. My brother has gone to the bank, and so we are alone. Selina will bring you rolls and honey or fresh fruit if you prefer and then we shall drink tea and you will tell me all about my Faisal. Zahra laughs at me, but a mother grows anxious for her only son, when he lives amongst strangers.'

Felicia could only sympathise. She missed Faisal already, and longed for his presence as a bulwark between herself and Raschid.

'It is a bad time for him to go to New York, just when you are visiting us,' Umm Faisal acknowledged, 'but Raschid thought it necessary.'

And Raschid's decisions must never be questioned, Felicia thought resentfully.

The fresh fruit and delicious warm rolls Selina brought helped to revive her, and after a refreshing shower Felicia dressed in a flattering ice blue linen skirt, attractively pleated at the front, a toning striped blouse, completing an outfit that was both cool and practical. The skirt had a matching jacket, but the morning was so warm that Felicia left it hanging in the wardrobe. Pale blue eye-shadow and soft pink lip-gloss gave her a hint of sophistication, building up her seriously depleted self-confidence.

With a good many nods and smiles Selina led her to Umm Faisal's private sitting room on the ground floor. The older woman was sitting cross-legged on the carpet, and she rose gracefully when Felicia entered. The room was cool and shadowy, a long divan beneath the iron grille of a window, heaped with cushions covered in vivid silks, the rich crimsons and peacock blues picked out in the jewel-coloured Persian carpet, a vibrant note of colour against the black and white tiled floor. On a small low table stood a brass samovar, bubbling gently, the scent of mint tea wafting towards Felicia as she crossed the room. Above the faint whirring of the air-conditioning she could hear the sound of birds singing.

'Raschid had an aviary built when we moved to this house,' Umm Faisal explained. 'It is pleasant to walk in the gardens in the evening and listen to their song.'

'I thought I heard fountains playing when we arrived

last night, and they sounded wonderful,' Felicia acknowledged.

'Ah yes. There is no sweeter sound to the Arab ear than that of water, and even now when we no longer need to fear the dry season I have to force myself not to waste a drop.' She shook her head. 'Old habits die hard, and Raschid is constantly chiding me for my folly. He bought this house for us when my husband died—Raschid really prefers the desert, but it is not safe to bring up children so far from medical care even in these days. He gave up much when Saud died—but then Faisal will have told you that.'

Had he? Felicia could remember well enough Faisal's complaints about his uncle. 'He must have been very young,' she murmured now involuntarily, referring to Raschid.

Umm Faisal smiled. 'Barely nineteen. He was the son of my father's second wife. My mother bore no sons to my father, so he took a second wife, but Yasmin was never truly happy. She was her parents' only child and had been educated in England according to her mother's wish. However, when it came to her marriage her father insisted that it must be in the old tradition. My father was her second cousin, but although she was a dutiful wife, she rarely smiled or laughed. She died when Raschid was three, and I have often wondered if she yearned for her mother's country. Raschid does not speak of it, but her death saddened him greatly. He has not had an easy life,' Umm Faisal continued quietly, 'and it is for this reason that I should like to see him settled with a family of his own.' She looked at Felicia with contemplative eyes. 'In Raschid East and West meet, and I know that he is sometimes impatient of our ways. It was his wish that Zahra and Nadia attend the university—and I think the English part of him yearns for a closer companionship with his wife than Moslem girls are taught to expect. It is for this reason, I think, that he had never taken a bride.'

She pitied the woman who eventually took him on, Felicia thought grimly, but naturally she did not voice these thoughts to her companion.

Today Umm Faisal was dressed in Eastern costume, and Felicia suspected that the Western garb of the previous evening had been donned merely to put her at her ease. Her heart warmed towards this tiny, plump woman whose ways were so very different from her own, but who was plainly willing to welcome her son's friends into her home. Remembering the gifts she had bought in London—still unpacked—Felicia was tempted to run upstairs and get them, but decided to wait until Zahra returned, knowing how the Arabs loved ceremony of any kind.

She tried not to feel too dismayed when Ali brought the Mercedes to the door later that afternoon, wishing that Umm Faisal was going with her.

The arrangement was that Ali would drive to the university to collect Zahra and then take both girls back to Kuwait town so that they could look at the shops at their leisure, but when they were driving through Kuwait, Felicia remembered that she had no Kuwaiti money and she persuaded Ali to drop her outside a bank and go on to collect Zahra without her.

'I shall wait for Zahra here', she assured the puzzled servant, gesturing to the large plate glass building behind her.

As she emerged from the interior of the car she was glad that she had changed her striped blouse for a thinner, sleeveless one, with a gently scooped neckline.

The bank cashier was politely helpful, patiently explaining the denominations of her Kuwaiti money and showing her the rate of exchange. He spoke excellent English, and although Felicia doubted that her few pounds would go very far, it was reassuring to have money in her purse.

She emerged from the welcome coolness of the bank into the harsh sunlight, fascinated by the panorama of life passing by in front of her while she waited for Ali to return with Zahra. Hawk-eyed, bronzed men in their white *dishdashes*; their robes immaculately clean, their headdresses held in place by glinting gold *igals*.

A group of old men sat cross-legged on the pavement, and to her amusement Felicia realised that they were watching a television in a shop window.

Although men were undeniably in the majority, she noticed several girls walking about unescorted, some even wearing jeans and blouses, but there were still plenty of women who retained the traditional black *burga*, veils covering their faces as they swayed gracefully in the wake of their men. The men were fascinating if one could overlook their intense chauvinism, Felicia reflected. Even in middle age they retained their upright carriage and good looks. Black eyes glittered curiously over her slender figure, hawk noses and thin lips a reminder of their heritage. It was impossible not to admire them in their strict adherence to their way of life, though she herself could never accept male superiority. Faisal was more gentle by nature, more malleable, ready to indulge and cosset her, the effect no doubt of his Western education, and a result of the close bond that evidently existed between him and his mother. Raschid was cast in a far different mould.

All too easy to imagine him staring down the length of his arrogant nose at some unfortunate female who had incurred his displeasure.

Ali was gone longer than she had anticipated, and she scoured the busy street looking for the familiar Mercedes. A group of youths were approaching her, their eyes bold and assessing, and Felicia was beginning to feel increasingly uncomfortable. So much so that she almost wished for the protection of the enveloping black garments of the other women to hide her from the openly lascivious glances she was attracting.

When she did see the Mercedes gliding to a halt several yards away, she started to hurry towards it, but it was not Ali who got out of the car. It was Raschid himself, his face dark and forbidding as he strode towards her, the thin silk of his shirt open at the neck to reveal the strong, tanned column of his throat. A tiny thread of awareness filtered through her dismay, coupled with the unwelcome admission that these olive-skinned men with their arrogant profiles and lean grace made their English counterparts seem pale and flabby in comparison. Her heart was beating uncomfortably fast, her pulses racing, her mouth dry with nervous fear. Instead of going to meet Raschid, she hung back, frozen to the spot like some poor little mouse, petrified by the cruel grace of the falcon on his downward swoop.

Dark fingers, like talons, gripped her arm, swinging her into shocked contact with a hard male body, the scent of male skin filling her nostrils as, momentarily, she was pressed against Raschid's lean length.

'Miss Gordon!' There was exasperation as well as tightly controlled anger in the two words, and Felicia found herself stammering weakly, searching for some means to dispel his wrath:

'I was waiting for Zahra.'

'Having told Ali to leave you, completely alone, in the middle of a strange city—Yes, I know,' he agreed grimly. 'Fortunately Ali had the good sense to come and tell me.' His eyes slid over her body; the fragile hip bones revealed by her clinging skirt; the slender curve of her waist below the unexpected fullness of her breasts. Aware of his regard, Felicia went hot and cold all over, suppressing the instinctive desire to conceal herself from him.

'In this country, Miss Gordon,' he told her, 'a woman of good family does not walk the streets alone, with her body on display for the delectation of all and sundry, to be gossiped over and speculated about, as those boys were discussing you. I tell you this—Faisal would not be pleased were he to learn of this escapade.'

Shocked into silence by the censorious words, Felicia bit hard on her lip.

'I just wanted to get some money,' she choked, nearly in tears, humiliated by the thought that Raschid was witnessing her distress.

'You could have applied to me,' Raschid's cold voice continued inexorably. 'Or does that much-flaunted liberation you European women are so fond of mean that you are unwilling even to do that!'

He made her sound so petty and childish that she could have wept. She had simply never thought of asking him to change her few travellers' cheques for her, but a corner of her mind acknowledged that he had some basis for his accusation, although stubbornly she resisted it.

'I'm sure it isn't a crime to walk alone—other women were doing so, and in European dress,' Felicia said defiantly.

Raschid snapped long fingers, ignoring the challenge in her eyes.

'Foreigners!' he announced contemptuously. 'Women whose families do not have a care for their reputation.'

'My reputation is my own,' Felicia snapped crossly. 'And I'm perfectly capable of taking care of it myself. After all, I've been living alone in London for the past five years.'

'In Kuwait, Miss Gordon, a woman's reputation is the concern of all her family, and a slur upon that reputation reflects upon all members of that family. Faisal may or may not have told you that Zahra is betrothed to a young man of exceptionally rigid family. The betrothal has only been settled after a good deal of very delicate negotiation. These are sensitive times where the Moslem religion is concerned. The information that a young woman attached to our family—in however nebulous a fashion— is disporting herself as you have been today could have very serious repercussions indeed where Zahra's future is concerned.'

If he expected her to be cowed and chastened then he had another think coming, Felicia fumed.

'An arranged marriage? How typical of you!' she stormed. 'If you had your way you would ruin Faisal's life in the same way, and then your life wouldn't be disturbed by an unwanted English girl whose morals and antecedents you so obviously suspect! I'm sorry to disappoint you, Sheikh Raschid, but I will marry Faisal, and there's nothing you can do to stop us, even if we do have to wait three years.'

She wondered if it was anger or disgust that made his mouth tighten so forbiddingly. No doubt in Kuwait, girls of good family did not state their intentions so openly, but waited with dutifully downcast eyes for their fathers and brothers to tell them whom they would marry. Poor Zahra! How did she feel about her arranged marriage?

The cruel fingers were still holding her prisoner, while relentless grey eyes swept her from head to foot and back again, so that she was reduced to trembling fury.

'Let me go!' she muttered. 'People are staring at us!'

'And that offends you?' His mouth thinned cruelly and for the first time she was aware of its full lower curve, indicating a passion she would have thought foreign to his nature.

'Do you realise that were you married to Faisal you would have just given him cause to divorce you twice over; firstly by disporting yourself as you did in the street for all to see, and secondly for allowing me to address you so intimately and in full view of anyone who cares to see? Faisal would not like that, Miss Gordon.'

She knew that it was true. There was a certain inflection in the younger man's voice whenever he mentioned his uncle that hinted at the beginnings of a jealousy which could easily be fanned from a small spark to a blazing conflagration.

'And *I* don't like being stared at as though I were on sale in the market place!' Felicia replied tartly, tearing her gaze away from the hypnotic effect of his cool stare.

'You surprise me. In one respect at least I cannot fault Faisal's judgement. You are an extremely beautiful woman, but it takes more than a desirable body and a pretty face to make a good wife.'

'Although they are admirable traits in a mistress? Is that what you mean?'

Raschid's eyebrows rose quellingly, adding to his formidable air of hauteur.

'I did not say so,' he replied positively. 'Was that your intention when you agreed to come out here? To sell yourself to the highest bidder, knowing that a wealthy Arab would pay well for that lissom white body you conceal so inadequately?'

She would have struck him there and then in the middle of the crowded thoroughfare if he had not transferred his grip from her arm to her wrist, pain stabbing through her tender flesh like a shock from red-hot wires at the ferocity of the fingers clamped round her frail bones.

'Why do you ask?' she cried bitterly. 'Are you thinking of putting in an offer yourself?'

She knew instantly that she had gone too far. His mouth tightened ominously, his eyes condemning as they swept her with thinly veiled contempt.

'No way,' he said cruelly, shaking his head. 'I don't buy soiled merchandise, Miss Gordon, desirable though it may be superficially. A chipped jade figurine, a flawed carpet, a second-hand woman, they are all worthless!'

His words left her gasping with mingled shock and rage. She tried to pull herself free and suffered the added indignity of being jerked against the hard length of his body, shock driving the breath out of her lungs as she bunched her muscles against the impact. The contact lasted only a second, but as she pulled away and stalked across the pavement to the car, where Zahra was staring curiously from the window, she felt as though the imprint of Raschid's flesh was burned against her own, and she, who had been held far closer to Faisal, wondered why she should have found that momentary contact with Raschid so intensely disturbing. Long strides brought the object of her tumultuous thoughts alongside her, lean fingers descending over hers, clinical eyes studying the way she flinched away as he grasped the car door, holding it open for her.

The entire episode could have lasted no longer than

the space of a few minutes, but Felicia felt for some reason as though it were one that she would never forget. Tense and defensive, she tried to calm her jangled nerves as Raschid closed the door and walked round to the front passenger seat.

Just for a second she had glimpsed the emotions Raschid concealed behind his cool façade, and what she had seen had frightened her. He was as different from Faisal as chalk from cheese, she reflected shakily. He had none of Faisal's gentle compassion; none of his boyish charm, so why should he linger in her thoughts when she badly needed to cling to the memory of Faisal's love?

CHAPTER FOUR

THERE was no opportunity for conversation on the return journey to the villa, although once or twice Felicia caught Zahra's sympathetic eyes on her in a way that made a mockery of her own hopes that the latter had not noticed her uncle's anger.

When the car stopped in the outer courtyard, she whispered gently to Felicia,

'Don't be too upset, I always hate it when Raschid is annoyed with me. That dreadful cold anger of his is far worse than if he actually lost his temper.'

Felicia was feeling far too ruffled to be soothed by the placatory words and only exclaimed shortly,

'Your uncle may take it upon himself to order your life, Zahra, but he will never order mine. If I want to walk the streets of Kuwait alone, then I shall do so!'

With that she stalked into the house, head held high, Zahra following hurriedly behind.

'He has made you very angry, hasn't he?' she sympathised.

'Angry?' Felicia almost choked in her indignation. 'He practically humiliated me! Treating me like . . .' She broke off. There was no point in trying to make Zahra understand her feelings. 'Oh, what's the use?' she said wearily. 'I'm only glad that once we're married, Faisal and I can go our own way. I would hate to live here under your uncle's roof!'

She sounded so bitter that Zahra frowned unhappily, touching her arm.

'Perhaps it is that Raschid does not understand, Felicia. If I were to tell him that you were upset. . . . Faisal would not have approved either, you know,' she added gently. 'I shall speak with Raschid . . .!'

'No! No, Zahra, don't do that.' In her mind Felicia
was thinking how badly she was failing in the mission
Faisal had set her, but Zahra misinterpreted her words,
and her face broke into a relieved smile.

'You are beginning to forgive Raschid already,' she
breathed. 'I *know* he didn't mean to upset you, Felicia.
He forgets sometimes how formidable he is!'

Like a falcon forgets its prey, Felicia thought bitterly.
Zahra saw her relative through rose-tinted glasses. Forgive
him indeed! That was something she would never do!
When she remembered what he had said about her, and
the look in his eyes. . . .

Her mother normally rested during the afternoon, Zahra
explained to Felicia as they went inside. It was a practice
she herself would probably want to adopt as the days grew
hotter, she added, and because of this it was the custom
that the family did not gather for their meal until early
evening.

After she had showered and slipped into a refreshingly
cool dress, Felicia inspected her reflection in the mirror.
Was her appearance 'chaste' enough to pass Raschid's
rigid specifications? she asked herself wryly. Her dress had
a gently rounded neckline and small puffed sleeves, the
neck and hem piped in crisp white scalloping in contrast
to the lemon-gold cotton. She had washed her hair and it
curled attractively on to her shoulders, more red than
gold in the fading light. A thin gold necklace drew attention to the slender column of her throat, a matching
bracelet round one delicate wrist, high-heeled, strappy
sandals completing her outfit.

For dinner they were served with roast lamb, deliciously flavoured with herbs, pastries stuffed with exotic
vegetables, and spicy rice dishes, and Felicia groaned a
little to think of the effect of all this rich food on her
figure.

When the first course had been cleared away, the maids
reappeared with an immense tray of fresh fruit, and more

of the frighteningly fattening almond and marzipan tartlets they had had the night before.

Felicia accepted a slice of melon and some fresh, sweet dates, noting that Raschid had the same although his sister and Zahra tucked into the almond tarts with a cheerful disregard for the consequences.

After the meal a manservant came in with coffee cups and an elegant silver coffee pot, pouring the thick, steaming liquid into the fragile cups and handing them round.

Felicia had brought her gifts downstairs and hidden them under her chair. She had intended to distribute them after the meal when, she hoped, Raschid would retire to his own quarters, but to her annoyance he seemed determined to linger, leaning back in his chair, with a tigerish grace she had never seen in a European, his hair blue-black under the light of the chandelier. She wondered if he had ever sat cross-legged in the tents of his tribe, eating from the communal dish and drinking from the communal cup as Arabian hospitality demanded. In his expensive hand-made silk suit he looked every inch the sophisticated businessman, but she sensed that under the suave façade lurked a man as elemental as the desert which was his natural home.

While Umm Faisal and Zahra chatted, Felicia's eyes strayed again and again to the shuttered face of the man seated opposite her. The betrayingly passionate curve of his lower lip caught her attention, as it had done before, and she shivered involuntarily, imagining what it would be like to feel that hard mouth against her own; that warm golden skin next to the creamy paleness of her own.

A shudder racked her. What on earth was she thinking? In vain she tried to conjure up the protective image of Faisal's softer features, as though they were a talisman to ward off the potent effect of Raschid's masculinity. What was wrong with her? she wondered despairingly; Raschid stood for everything she most despised, and yet here she was comparing him to Faisal, and finding the harsh features had somehow insinuated themselves into her memory, superimposed over Faisal's more gentle image. It was not to be tolerated. In vain she tried to recall Faisal's warm smile and liquid eyes, but as though he had worked a spell upon her, all she got back was a mirror image of Raschid's cold grey eyes and derisory smile. Like one in a trance she tried to shake off her tormenting thoughts, dismayed by her momentary awareness of the man seated across from her. Hurriedly she bent down to retrieve her gaily wrapped packages, her colour high.

'I've brought you both a little something from England—a small token of my gratitude for your hospitality.'

Umm Faisal inclined her head graciously, but Zahra was far less inhibited.

'A present?' she exclaimed with shining eyes. 'Oh, Felicia, how lovely—but you shouldn't have.'

'Nothing very exciting, I'm afraid.' Felicia warned her, remembering the deprecatory words Faisal always used before giving her some shockingly extravagant treat. It was an Arab trait to deprecate their possessions, stemming from the days when to boast of one's achievements could call down the 'evil eye' upon the bragger, and she knew it was still the custom for an Arab to welcome a visitor to his 'humble' home, even if that home were a palace.

A little apprehensively she watched Zahra open her present, but the younger girl's gasp of pleasure obliterated her fears that it would not be well received. Even Raschid was commanded to admire the contents of the make-up box, although he did so with typical male indulgence for so purely a female delight.

Umm Faisal's pleasure was a little more restrained, but genuine none the less, and Felicia was pleased that she had taken the trouble to ask Faisal what sort of perfume his mother preferred.

'It's gorgeous!' Zahra exclaimed, sniffing the bottle. 'It reminds me of the one al-Azir mixed for you the last time we were in Jeddah, Mother—do you remember?'

'I certainly do,' Raschid interrupted drily. 'It was

extremely expensive.'

Felicia smiled politely at his little joke, and looked up to find Zahra watching her expectantly.

'Where is Raschid's present, Felicia? Or are you keeping it from him until he apologises for this afternoon?' she teased with a smile.

Felicia felt her colour come and go. How could she say that she had not brought a present for Raschid? She bit her lip and then remembered the paperweight she had bought for Nadia, Faisal's elder sister.

'It's upstairs,' she improvised hurriedly, hating the guilty blush that mantled her cheeks. 'I wasn't sure that Raschid would be eating with us.'

'You have forgiven him, then. I knew you would. Do go and get it.' Zahra urged Felicia, before turning to her mother, her eyes twinkling. 'Uncle Raschid was unkind to Felicia this afternoon, Mother. She didn't realise she could have asked him to cash her travellers' cheques and she had gone into the bank *alone*!'

The shocked expression on Umm Faisal's face told Felicia that Raschid had spoken no less than the truth when he warned her about her behaviour, and she used the diversion created by Zahra's announcement to excuse herself and slip upstairs to collect the paperweight.

Fortunately it had been wrapped in a silvery striped paper suitable for either sex, and hating herself for the deceit, she hurried downstairs with the small package. When she had decided against bringing a gift for Faisal's uncle, she had not bargained for being faced with a situation such as this evening's!

As she handed Raschid the small square box her fingers trembled, accidentally brushing his, the brief contact sending alarm bells jangling along her nervous system, her eyes wide and dismayed in her small heart-shaped face. She knew that it was too much to hope that the man thanking her so urbanely for her thoughtfulness had not noticed the small, betraying gesture.

Nothing escaped those smoky-grey eyes, now sardonic

with comprehensive amusement, and Felicia slipped hurriedly back into her chair, wishing that she had waited
for a more propitious moment for her present giving.

'Go on, then, open it!' Zahra commanded her uncle,
her eyes on the package. 'I'm dying to see what it is!'

'Then I had better unwrap it quickly, before Miss
Gordon accuses me of further cruelty to my family,' was
Raschid's cool comment as lean fingers made nonsense of
the sealing.

When the paper fell away to reveal the dark blue
leather box, Zahra expelled an impatient sigh.

'Raschid, do hurry—it looks very exciting!'

In the growing darkness of the Oriental room with its
plain white walls and luxurious, richly coloured Persian
carpets; its priceless antique furniture with its glowing
patina, the pure beauty of the blue-green glass was a
poignant reminder to Felicia of the country she had left
behind. The glass was Caithness, from Scotland, where
craftsmen took a pride in fashioning the heavy paper-
weights, imprisoning within the depths of the molten glass,
small flowers; petals; sea anemones so that their beauty
would live for ever. The one Felica had chosen held a
blue-green sea anemone, and it had been one of a limited
range and consequently frighteningly expensive, but she
had fallen in love with its cool, remote beauty.

As she watched, her breath caught in her throat,
Raschid lifted it out of its white satin bed, balancing it on
his open palm. The silence that followed was a tribute to
the craftsmen who had conceived and made it.

'It's beautiful,' Zahra whispered, touching it with a
delicate forefinger. 'So cool and fresh—like you, Felicia.'

'It is a gift any Arab would treasure, Miss Gordon,'
Raschid's deep voice agreed. 'The glassblower has
captured the quality and colour of the sea in our gulf,
and nothing is more precious to our race than water.'

'It can be used as an ink-holder, or just a paperweight,'
Felicia told them, dismayed by the faint huskiness in her
voice. For some subtle reason which she could not define,

the gift had taken on an intensely personal aura she had never intended it to have. When she bought it the salesgirl told her that it was designed to be used as an ink-holder or perfume bottle, and it was for the latter reason that she had deemed it suitable for Nadia, apart from its obvious beauty. Thank goodness she had not bought her perfume, she decided, quelling a nervous giggle; then she would have been placed in an embarrassing position. If she had not been so stubbornly against buying anything for Raschid in the first place, she would not now be in this unpleasant situation, she reminded herself, trying not to notice Raschid's cool scrutiny both of her and the gift.

'You are very generous,' he said at last, silvery-grey eyes holding anxious green ones. 'More generous than I deserve.' He placed the paperweight back in its box, snapped the lid down and got up. 'If you will excuse me, there are certain business matters I have to attend to.'

Felicia had wanted to enquire whether there were any letters for her. She had learned from Zahra that all the mail, irrespective of its eventual recipient, was passed to Raschid, and she was hoping that there might be a letter for her from Faisal. Although she had only been in Kuwait a very short time, Faisal had not written to her since his departure for New York, and she had half expected to find a letter awaiting her arrival. A letter from him would help banish the memory of those tension-fraught seconds when awareness of Raschid had threatened to swamp her, and she badly needed the reassurance that hearing from him would bring.

'How clever of you to choose such marvellous presents,' Zahra murmured admiringly later. 'Especially Raschid's. Did Faisal tell you that he collected rare glass?'

Felicia shook her head. There seemed to be rather a lot of things Faisal had neglected to tell her about his uncle, and she guessed intuitively that these omissions had been deliberate.

'You are showing *siyasa* after all, Felicia,' Zahra

dimpled up at her. 'Your generosity will surely melt Raschid's heart.'

That was the last thing it was likely to do, Felicia thought despairingly. If Raschid thought that she was deliberately trying to soften his hostility he would be less likely than ever to view her in a favourable light.

'It is my name day soon,' Zahra confided. 'Raschid has promised that we may go to the oasis for a few days. You will like it. I don't expect I will be able to spend much time there once I am married, as it is really Raschid's house, so this is by way of being a special treat.'

It was the first time Zahra had mentioned her marriage and Felicia did not like to pry. However, they were alone, Umm Faisal having excused herself, and Zahra seemed to be in the mood for confidences. 'They brought the material for my wedding gown this afternoon,' she told Felicia, wrinkling her nose slightly. 'Of course, I am not supposed to know anything about it.'

'Don't you mind marrying a stranger?' Felicia asked curiously, hoping that she wasn't treading on dangerous ground, for she had no wish to upset the younger girl.

Zahra looked shocked and indignant.

'Saud is not a stranger! Whatever gave you that idea?' She shook her head.

Feeling rather perplexed, Felicia ventured hesitantly, 'But when your uncle mentioned to me the negotiations I thought your marriage must be an arranged one.'

Zahra laughed. 'Well, yes, in a way I suppose it is. Saud and I met at the university, but his family is a very important one and very old-fashioned. Saud was to have married his first cousin, as is customary, but fortunately Raschid was able to discover that the girl wanted to marry elsewhere, and so he was able to persuade Saud's family to accept me as Saud's wife. It could have been very difficult, for it would have been an unforgivable insult were Saud to refuse to marry his cousin, and conversely, had the girl objected to him, it would have caused her father to lose face. Our wedding is to take place quite soon, but first must come the formal visits.' She pulled a face. 'It is all so silly really, both of us having to pretend that we don't know one another. I would be quite happy to get married in your English fashion, but Raschid says that sometimes the more roundabout route is actually the shorter.'

Felicia did not know what to say. She had imagined that Zahra was being forced into the marriage for reasons of policy and had even suspected that somehow or other Raschid would benefit financially from the marriage. Now she was being compelled to review her suspicions.

'Of course Saud's family demanded a very large dowry,' Zahra continued matter-of-factly, startling her still further. 'But Raschid has been very generous. You must ask Mother to show you my bridal chest. It will hold Saud's gifts to me on our marriage, and it has been passed down through our family for ten generations.'

Felicia was still digesting this unwelcome insight into Raschid's actions when Zahra excused herself, saying that she had some studying to do. When she had gone Felicia stared out into the darkness of the gardens. It seemed that she had completely misunderstood Raschid's motives—at least as far as Zahra was concerned, for there could be no mistaking his attitude towards her. Was inviting her here a roundabout way to destroying Faisal's love for her? With considerable misgivings she wandered restlessly from the window to the door leading out into the courtyard, tempted by its inviting solitude and fresh air. It was cooler outside than she had expected and she shivered in her thin dress, but the music of the fountains was particularly haunting by night, suiting her mood, and she found herself drawn to where the clean, cool water splashed down into its marble pool. She passed the birds in their aviary and sighed faintly. She was as much a prisoner as they, although there were no walls to her cage other than custom and hostility.

'Miss Gordon!'

She froze as the dark shadow loomed over her, the sound of her name on those cruel lips sending shivers of apprehension running over her skin. All at once the velvet darkness seemed to press down on her, every instinct warning her to flee as Raschid emerged from the shadows, crossing the courtyard with silent stealth.

She had thought that she had the courtyard to herself, Raschid the last person she had expected to materialise at her side, and she choked back her dismay, forcing herself to say coolly, 'Sheikh—I didn't see you. Zahra told me you'd gone out.'

'So I had,' he agreed, 'But now I have returned, and like you I was tempted into the garden to enjoy its solitude.'

Felicia turned, intending to return to the protection of the house, but his fingers grasped her shoulder, forcing her to stand mute under his considering scrutiny. His eyes seemed to strip away her fragile defences, leaving her exposed and vulnerable, her eyes wide and uncertain as she tried to hold his gaze.

'This meeting is most opportune,' he drawled at length. 'I am glad of the chance to speak privately with you.'

'I thought my presence was yours to command,' Felicia retorted bitterly. 'Or is the Arabian male no longer master in his own house?'

He ignored her taunt, his eyes mocking as they pierced the darkness. 'I was thinking of your embarrassment and my sister's curiosity were I to send for you privately; not my own ability to command you if I so wished. Fatima tells me that Zahra was to have shown you the town this afternoon, and apparently my appearance on the scene deprived you of this treat.'

When Felicia refused to reply he continued coolly·

'That being the case, I shall put myself at your disposal later in the week. You know, of course, that Friday is our holy day, but if you will name another, I shall make sure that it is free.'

Munificence indeed, Felicia thought wryly, but being escorted around Kuwait by a disapproving Raschid was the last thing she wanted.

'There's no need for you to go to such trouble,' she assured him quickly—too quickly, she realised, when she saw him curse under his breath, his fingers tightening painfully.

'It seems that you are determined to quarrel with me,' he accused. 'You British have a saying that is particularly relevant to us Arabs, and I suggest that you accept the olive branch I extend. We are extremely dependent upon the olive in our harsh climate, and we never take its name in vain. It is plain that Zahra has taken you to her heart— perhaps the fault for this is mine in not warning her more thoroughly about the type of woman you are—However, the damage is now done, and it will hurt her if she sees that we are enemies. She is to leave us soon, and I will not have her last days with her family spoiled and marred by ill-feeling between us.'

'A pity you didn't think of that before you insulted me so grossly this afternoon,' Felicia reminded him bleakly, dismayed by the bitterness that swept over her.

'So!' He seemed to consider her for a moment, his eyes probing the darkness until she shrank under their assessing gleam. 'Very well. If I cannot gain your co-operation through goodwill, I shall have to gain it in some other fashion.'

A frisson of fear ran over her skin. In the dark the fountain played, but the sound suddenly seemed heightened to her overstrung nerves, emphasising the solitude of the garden.

'If you're thinking of bribery,' she said distastefully, 'I suggest you think again. There's nothing you could offer me that would change my love for Faisal.'

'Nothing?' Raschid taunted softly, coming towards her like a jungle cat, all feline grace and terrifying danger. Although it was dark she could see the faint sheen of his skin, marred by the dark shadow of his beard along his jawline. It was unfair that any man should possess such arrogant certainty of his own power to compel others to do his bidding, she thought nervously, her tongue wetting her dry lips, as long lashes flicked down over his eyes, hiding his thoughts from her. His touch had become less brutal, his fingers gently massaging the fragile bones of her shoulders, sending a warning screaming through her veins. This man is dangerous, it seemed to say, and with trembling certainty she knew that she had pulled the tiger's tail and must surely suffer the consequences.

Without her being able to do a thing about it, Raschid slid his hands from her shoulders to her waist, propelling her towards him, his voice a mocking imitation of tenderness, as he murmured softly against her hair, 'You leave me with very little choice, Miss Gordon. You have continually defied me, and must pay the price. You cannot expect me to believe you are naïve enough not to know how a man will retaliate when you challenge his most basic instincts?

'Very well then,' he said harshly, when she refused to answer, 'let this be your punishment.'

Cruel hands imprisoned her against the hard warmth of his body, his voice cold as he commanded her to abandon her vain struggles to be free, as his mouth descended on hers with a punishing ferocity.

If she had once read passion into that full underlip, there was none now. It was a kiss of bitter anger; a contemptuous punishment of her defiance, breaking through the fragile cobweb dreams she had spun of a moment like this; alone in an Eastern dusk, in the arms of a man who could trace his origins back to the fierce tribesmen who called the whole desert home. But then, of course, she had been thinking of Faisal—not this man who crushed her against the steel wall of his chest, without a thought for the fragility of her own soft curves; who destroyed her dreams as easily as he might tear the wings from a foolish moth.

Furiously resentful, she withstood the harsh pressure of his mouth; rigidly refusing to admit defeat, her lips clamped shut against the demand of his. He might be able to physically restrain her, but nothing could make her respond to him in the way he had obviously intended.

The kiss could only have lasted seconds, but it seemed an eternity before she was released, feeling mangled like some poor creature set free from the talons of the falcons that sheikhs flew from their wrists.

She beat at his chest with ineffectual hands, but he grasped her wrists, smiling down tauntingly.

'Well, do you still say that you can defy me?'

'I'll tell Faisal what you've done!' Felicia all but wept, trembling with humiliation, but Raschid only laughed.

'You would never dare,' he told her softly. 'We have a saying in our country, that it takes two to commit adultery. Mud sticks, Miss Gordon. By all means tell Faisal. I wish you would . . .!'

Leaving her to digest that remark, he released her so suddenly that she almost fell. Her fingers went instinctively to her throbbing lips, tears blurring her vision.

'Oh, by the way,' Raschid added casually, slipping a hand into his jacket and withdrawing the blue leather box that held the paperweight, 'I suggest you give this to the person for whom it was originally intended.' And he threw the box towards her. 'I think we both of us know that you would never have bought such a gift for me, and you insult my intelligence by expecting me to believe that you did. Keep it for Faisal. I am sure he will be far more appreciative—and show it in a more acceptable way!'

He had gone before Felicia could admit that the paperweight had been purchased for Nadia, his anger leaving an almost tangible atmosphere in the cool garden.

He had shamed and humiliated her; mocked her love for Faisal and his for her, and treated her in a way that no Arab should ever treat a female member of his family, and yet try as she might she could not conjure up the comforting memory of how it felt to be in Faisal's arms, and it came to her, with shock, that although he had driven her to fury and bitter despair she had not shrunk under Raschid's embrace as she did when with Faisal.

Because she had been too angry, she assured herself, staring down at the box in her hand.

Suddenly she hated the paperweight more than she had
ever hated anything in her life. Before she could change
her mind she hurled the box as far as she could, barely
aware of the small, distant thud as it fell amongst some
roses, then she turned her back on the courtyard and
sought the sanctuary of her bedroom.

Under the electric light she saw the faint beginnings of
what would eventually be bruises from Raschid's tight
grip.

Removing her clothes, she showered, soaping her flesh
until it glowed, as though by doing so she could remove
for all time the memory of Raschid's kiss. She hated him!
Hated him, she told her flushed reflection defiantly. So
why was she crying, silly, weak tears, that would only had
afforded her self-confessed enemy the greatest satisfaction?

She touched a tear-damp cheek with shaking fingers.
In the space of a few earth-shaking minutes Raschid had
destroyed her illusions and ripped away the veils of innocence which had hitherto protected her, and all because
she had dared to flout his authority and walk unattended
in the streets of Kuwait.

But as she waited for sleep to claim her, Felicia
admitted that it went deeper than that. For the first time
in her life she had experienced true fear, and as her eyes
closed she fought desperately to remember what it had
felt like to be held in Faisal's arms, investing her memories
with a passion they had never possessed in an endeavour
to obliterate every last trace of Raschid's touch.

CHAPTER FIVE

FEMALE voices rose and fell, punctuated with laughter and the rattle of coffee cups. Umm Faisal had invited her friends round to meet Felicia, and judging by the number of women crowded into the room, Felicia suspected that her hostess numbered the entire town amongst her acquaintances.

Most of the visitors were of Umm Faisal's generation, and from an upstairs window Felicia had seen them hurrying from opulent cars, their bodies draped in heavy black cloaks, glancing neither to the left nor the right. Once inside, though, the cloaks were discarded like so many unwanted chrysalises to reveal Paris couture fashions and jewellery to rival the contents of the Tower of London.

From her cross-legged position on a damask cushion Felicia listened to her neighbour describing a recent visit to America. All the women spoke English, although sometimes with accents which made it almost impossible for her to recognise her native tongue.

This was the first time she had observed the formal ritual of receiving guests, Arab fashion; the gracious welcome and lavish hospitality; and above all the enthusiasm with which the visitors greeted her. Most of them had visited London at one time or another, and they all displayed an almost childlike curiosity about her life there, marvelling over the strange freedom European males allowed their women.

The maid, Selina, came round with fresh coffee, and Felicia sighed. Her stomach was awash with the bitter liquid, but since no one else seemed to be refusing, she felt she could hardly do so herself. Umm Faisal caught her eye, smiling understandingly. She whispered something to

75

Selina and to Felicia's relief the dusky serving girl passed by without filling her delicate porcelain cup.

Marble floors, and damask cushions; they were a far cry from her small bedsit with its second-hand furniture. Felicia found that she no longer thought of the austerity of plain white walls as a strange contrast to the luxurious silks and satins the Arabs used for furnishings. She had grown used to seeing Umm Faisal sitting cross-legged on a cushion on the floor, although most of the rooms were furnished in a more Western style, but she doubted if she could ever come to terms with the segregation of male and female; the absolute and all-embracing dominance of the male. However, Zahra told her that even this was less strictly adhered to than had once been the case, and she was forced to admit that where his family were concerned, Raschid was a very forward-thinking man indeed. A pity that his enlightened views did not extend to include her!

Someone knocked on the door, and instantly women were reaching for their veils, without haste or pretension, slipping them into place, as Selina opened the door. Servants, Zahra had told Felicia, did not need to veil.

'It is the Master, *sitti*,' the girl told Umm Faisal.

'Ah, yes, he has come to collect you, Felicia. Raschid is going to show Felicia Kuwait,' she explained for the benefit of her guests, adding something in Arabic that brought a twinkle to more than one pair of dark eyes.

'She says that it is as well that Raschid is a man of impeccable honour,' Felicia's companion whispered. 'In our day such a thing would not have been allowed, but times change.' She shrugged as though to say who was to tell whether or not such changes were for the better, laughing when Felicia got unsteadily to her feet. No wonder these women were so graceful and fluid; their limbs would be trained from childhood to accept such a pose, while hers protested agonisingly, pins and needles stabbing painfully through both feet.

After their confrontation in the garden, Felicia had never expected that Raschid would pursue his promise to take her sightseeing—if indeed a 'promise' it had been—but pride would not let her back down and refuse to go with him.

She had dressed for Umm Faisal's guests with special care, but as she opened the door, the horrible thought struck her that Raschid might think that she had donned her attractive outfit for his benefit.

She was wearing a peach linen suit, perfect with her warm colouring, a simple cream silk blouse underneath the neatly fitting jacket. Cream shoes and a slim clutch bag toned perfectly with subtle peach linen, and thin gold bangles chimed musically as she moved. They had been a gift from Faisal, and one which she had tried to refuse until he told her that unless she accepted them the bracelets would be thrown away. She thought of the emerald ring he had bought her—now with him in New York—and his anger when she had refused to wear it until his family accepted their engagement. Now, when it was too late, she wished she had brought the ring with her. Perhaps the sight of it might help to restore some of the high hopes with which she had come to Kuwait.

In Eastern garments she knew that she could never hope to rival the grace of girls who had been wearing them from babyhood, but as she glanced in the full-length mirror set into the wall, she reflected that she had every reason to feel pleased with her appearance, and knowing that she looked her best lent an air of confidence that bloomed in the soft colour of her cheeks and the warm glow of her eyes.

Today she had overcome an important hurdle. Umm Faisal's friends had accepted her, despite the differences in their cultures—East and West could blend happily, no matter what Raschid said. With the light of battle in her eyes, Felicia went to meet the man waiting for her in the paved courtyard.

Dim light filtered in through the tall narrow windows of the entrance hall, and at first she could not see him. Then he moved and she caught the white flash of his shirt, the cuffs immaculate as he shot one back to glance at his watch. The gesture, so typically male, made her smile, and that was when he turned and saw her, poised in the doorway, the dark wood a perfect foil for her translucent beauty, laughter trembling the generous curve of her mouth, her eyes calm and composed.

He came towards her, his expression unreadable. This time Felicia was determined to retain the upper hand.

'I'm sorry if I kept you waiting,' she apologised formally, 'but your sister's friends. . . .'

'You have no need to explain the female of the species to me, Miss Gordon. I'm perfectly conversant with its addiction to senseless chatter.'

His arrogance all but took her breath away.

'If it's senseless, it's because men like you refuse to give them the opportunity to be anything else,' she retorted, the serenity dying out of her eyes to be replaced by anger, but Raschid merely looked amused.

'Is that what you have been doing? Lecturing Fatima's guests on the rights of the liberated woman? You will not be very popular with their husbands, Miss Gordon.'

'I don't care whether I am or not,' Felicia announced recklessly.

'Foolish of you,' was Raschid's only comment. 'For those same husbands have the power to forbid their wives to have anything to do with you, if they wish, and Faisal would not approve of that. He may appear Westernised to you, Miss Gordon, but he will expect his wife to adhere to the rules of his own society, I assure you.'

Ignoring the warning, Felicia tossed her head, walking past Raschid to where the car was parked. Where once she had wanted to gain his approval for Faisal's sake, now she seemed to derive intense satisfaction from deliberately needling him—a trait so alien to her personality that she wondered a little bitterly why it had to be Faisal's guardian of all people who should arouse it within her.

'Faisal and I will not be living in Kuwait,' she told

Raschid, remembering what Faisal had said.

'No?' His sideways glance was mocking. 'Aren't you forgetting something, Miss Gordon?'

She refused to look at him, preceding him across the courtyard, where the scent of early roses already hung intoxicatingly on the warm air.

'If I am I'm sure you'll remind me of it.'

'Exactly so,' Raschid agreed urbanely. 'As an employee of the bank—and make no mistake, Faisal *is* an employee—he has a duty to go where the Board decides he will be of most use.'

'The Board?' Felicia queried bitterly. 'Don't you mean yourself?'

'In these circumstances I think I can agree that the two are synonymous.'

His suave satisfaction jarred, like a nerve in an aching tooth probed by an unwary tongue. Felicia hesitated, on the point of refusing to accompany him, but then she remembered Zahra's approaching birthday, and accepted that there would probably be no other suitable opportunity to buy her a present. Swallowing the words, with her pride, she contented herself with a cold glare in Raschid's direction.

For the last few days the household had gone busily frantic over the arrangements for transporting Umm Faisal, Raschid, Zahra and herself, as well as the staff and everything that they would require, to the oasis for the duration of the birthday celebrations. Only that morning Zahra had laughingly confided that without Raschid to master-mind the move she doubted if they would get any farther than Kuwait City. Felicia had suggested rather hesitantly that perhaps she ought to return home, in case her presence at such a time proved to be a nuisance, but Zahra's swift dismay soon reassured her. In point of fact, she and Zahra had become very close, and it was only her growing affection for the younger girl that prevented Felicia from giving full rein to her growing antipathy towards Raschid. As he had so rightly said, it would hurt Zahra if she thought they were quarrelling, and Felicia had as little desire to cast a blight over the birthday festivities as Raschid. For that reason an uneasy—on her part at least—truce had developed between them.

'A wise decision,' Raschid drawled suddenly, startling her. She glared at him suspiciously, caught off guard when he said smoothly, 'Don't bother denying that you were contemplating refusing my company. I dislike liars almost as much as I despise fortune-hunters.'

The sheer rage engendered by his dismissive tones rendered her speechless, totally unable to retaliate, and it wasn't until he walked round to the opposite side of the parked car and opened the driver's door that Felicia realised that Ali would not be accompanying them. Raschid leaned across the passenger seat, unlocking the door and pushing it open.

'I think I would prefer to sit in the back,' she said stiffly. 'Isn't that what all good Arab women do—dutifully take a back seat and leave the driving to their lords and masters?'

'On this occasion I think we will opt for the Western custom,' Raschid replied drily. 'Otherwise I shall be endangering both our lives by constantly having to look over my shoulder to converse with you—Or do you perhaps read a more sinister purpose into my request? Your imagination runs away with you, Miss Gordon.'

If anything his voice had become even more cuttingly unkind, and Felicia flushed painfully, knowing he was deliberately taunting her.

'Even if such was my desire,' he continued, 'which most assuredly it is not, I never, but never make love on the open carriageway between my home and the city. Kuwaiti drivers are not the most polite in the world, nor the most tolerant of dawdlers, as you will soon discover. I am sorry if I don't match up to the prowess of your previous escorts in this regard, but in the East we prefer to suit the activity to our surroundings.'

Felicia stood by the car, longing to slam the door shut, wishing she could think of a suitably cutting retort to burst for once and for all the complacent arrogance with which Raschid surrounded himself. She had forgotten that even though she was standing by the side of the Mercedes, Raschid could still read her expression quite accurately in the driving mirror, and she jumped when he drawled mockingly, 'I can almost feel the knife entering my heart, Miss Gordon. Be careful. In this country we believe in taking a life for a life.'

'Heart? What heart?' she retorted, too furious to pay much attention to the rest of the sentence. 'You don't possess such a thing, Sheikh Raschid!'

'Get in the car, Miss Gordon, and save your anger to fuel something more profitable than pitting your wits against mine.'

The arrogance of it! Felicia seethed as she slid into the seat, ignoring his smile as he leaned across her to close the door. At such close quarters an aura of taut masculinity emanated from him. She was pulsatingly aware of the warm sheen of his skin, drawn tightly over the narrow bones of his face; the way his eyelashes lay, long and dark against the sculptured bone; silk against satin, she thought irrelevantly, shiveringly aware of him in a way that she had never been aware of Faisal, but underneath lay a core of pure steel.

'Do I pass muster?'

She flushed as vividly as the roses blooming in the inner courtyard, hating to be caught out paying him any attention, no matter what the reason—and in this case, pure curiosity had drawn her eyes to his face, unwilling admiration keeping them there to wonder at the perfect symmetry of the bone structure underlying the smooth skin, even while the arrogant profile made her anger rise like a river in a flash flood, coming out of nowhere to appal her with its ferocity. How strange it was that a mingling of East and West should have produced this lordly, sensual man, while Faisal's pure Arab blood had produced a man in a much softer mould.

While she battled with her anger, she told herself that for Faisal's sake she must learn to tame it, to sit meek and docile under the razor-sharp tongue and probing glance. She had once read that a falcon could focus on its prey from many thousands of feet above it in the sky; so it was with Raschid. Those grey eyes held all the latent power of a modern laser beam.

They took the coast road. The day was deliciously warm, the merest breath of fresh air from the air-conditioning fanning her hair as they sped towards the city. The leather seats reclined to contour the body, and the radio emitted soothing music, but Felicia could not relax. She was as tense as a coiled spring, unwittingly betraying her anxiety in her tightly clenched fists.

'Relax,' Raschid surprised her by saying. 'Or is it merely the fact that you are a passenger rather than the driver which makes you so tense? How you European women rob yourselves of your very femininity by insisting on doing everything for yourselves!'

'Perhaps because our experience of your sex has taught us how unwise it is for us to rely on them for anything,' Felicia retorted unwisely, thinking of Uncle George, and how selfishly he had refused to allow either her aunt or herself the slightest little pleasure, begrudging every small thing he had done for them.

'Is that why you want to marry Faisal?' Raschid asked astutely. 'Because you see in him a shoulder on which to lean? Strange—I had not thought of you as a clinging vine; I see I shall have to revise my strategy. Clinging vines are notoriously difficult to remove, but Faisal is weak, Miss Gordon; whoever marries him will need to be mother, lover, and even jailer at times. Are you sure you are able to fulfil all those roles?'

'It's easy to list his failings when he's not here to defend himself,' Felicia retorted hotly, trying not to acknowledge the truth of what Raschid had said. Hadn't she sometimes noticed an inclination to adopt the role of helpless little boy by Faisal, when all was not going his way?

'You are loyal at least,' Raschid responded in clipped accents, as though the admission displeased him, then changed the subject to draw her attention to the British Embassy. Because he hoped that she would soon be entering that building, asking to be sent home, all her dreams of marriage to Faisal turned to so much dust.

Not for the first time Felicia wondered at her own foolish impetuosity in allowing Faisal to persuade her to come to Kuwait. He had paid for her air ticket; her own slender savings had gone on her new wardrobe, but Faisal had glibly assured her that it would not be long before he was able to join her in Kuwait, taking it for granted that she would remain with his family until their marriage. If that was not to take place until he was twenty-five she would have to return to England. Which meant that she would have to write and ask Faisal for the money for her ticket, for she was convinced that Raschid would never allow him to return to Kuwait while she was there.

As soon as Zahra's birthday was over she would write to him, she promised herself, comforted by this gesture of independence.

They drove past the Sief Palace, where guards stood stiffly to attention. A flag flew from the tall, square clock tower.

'His Highness the Emir is holding his *majlis*,' Raschid told her. 'In this country even the poorest amongst us can seek audience with the Emir to air his grievances if he so desires.'

'As long as *he* is male,' Felicia could not resist retorting.

'You seem to have an outsize chip on your shoulder regarding my sex, Miss Gordon—or is it that having gained your independence, you find you no longer want it?'

Felicia turned away from the malice-spiked glance. She had never been an advocate of Women's Lib, being quite happy to play the role for which nature had intended her; a role which she did not in any way consider to be subservient, however, so she now found herself saying quite heatedly, 'You do not deny that in your country women are of inferior status?'

'And that arouses your crusading instinct? Would it surprise you to know that women do have rights here; that they can complain to the Emir and even have their marriages set aside if they do not feel they are being treated properly? Perhaps the fact that they seldom do so tells its own story.'

'Or highlights the iniquities of their situation,' Felicia responded briefly, looking away, suddenly conscious of the insolent appraisal of narrowed grey eyes.

Raschid swung the car over, throwing her heavily against him, his arm brushing against her breasts and leaving her tingling with an awareness she had never experienced in Faisal's arms. What was this tension that seemed to vibrate in the air whenever she was near him? Whatever it was she did not like it.

'We are now entering the main *souk* and banking area, Miss Gordon,' Raschid informed her. 'I suggest that I park the car so that we can do the rest of our tour at a more leisurely pace.'

They left the car in a huge underground car-park beneath a towering plate glass and chrome office block.

'This is where we have our head office,' Raschid explained. 'In fact this building was one of our first ventures into the construction industry.'

'But not your last,' Felicia commented, remembering Faisal saying that the Bank had helped to finance the building of a hotel, amongst other things.

Raschid's hand was under her arm, a courtesy she had not expected, and she stumbled slightly as they emerged into the bright sunlight, his hard body taking the full impact of her tensed slenderness as they collided. Even that brief contact was enough to disturb her; the grey eyes cynically amused as they took in her flushed cheeks and angry eyes.

'No, not our last,' he agreed. 'Although this particular

venture was extremely profitable. As I am sure you already know, construction finance accounts for some forty per cent of our profits.' He looked at her averted profile, and gave her another thin-lipped smile.

'Am I boring you? Surely not. It is my experience that most women find the making of money almost as absorbing as the spending of it.'

'Well, I'm not most women,' Felicia replied shortly, pulling up with a start as they rounded a corner.

The wide street in front of them was laid out with trees and flower beds, greenery and tropical colour rioting everywhere. Where once there had been barren desert, fountains played, and instead of walking beneath the scorching glare of the sun, cool shady trees spread their green cloak invitingly over the strolling shoppers.

'Kuwait's Bond Street,' Raschid offered sardonically, as Felicia stared at the bewilderingly exotic display of precious stones in a jeweller's window.

'I have no doubt that you would far rather tour this area in Faisal's company than mine,' he drawled coolly, intimating that Faisal could have been persuaded to do more than merely glance disparagingly at the glittering diamond display that commanded the front of the window.

'I *would* have preferred to. But not for the reasons you suppose,' Felicia stressed pointedly, peering a little closer into the plate glass in the hope of finding something a little more modestly priced that she could buy for Zahra. Already she had learned of the younger girl's love of jewellery, and she smiled a little as she contemplated her reaction to the display of gems in front of her. She gave a faint sigh. There was nothing here to suit her slender pocket, and the shops, although luxuriously expensive, were disappointingly Westernised.

'What did you expect?' Raschid asked in thinly veiled amusement when she ventured to say as much. '*Souks* in the traditional manner, complete with beggars with alms bowls? There are no beggars in Kuwait these days, Miss

Gordon, unless it is by choice. At one time the blind men
of the city were employed to call the muezzin from the
minarets, lest strange male eyes perceived an unveiled
woman—such are the wonders of modern science that
nowadays the minaret towers are fitted with loudspeakers
which do the job far more effectively, and our poor, supported by the State, despise such modest work.'

'Blind men were deliberately employed for such a purpose?'

Intrigued despite her hostility, Felicia hesitated, to turn
an enquiring face up to the saturnine dark one above her.

'You find such safeguarding of the modesty of our
women amusing, I am sure. But not so long ago for a
man to look upon the face of another's wife was a gross
insult to them both—in your country a worse crime than
sleeping with one's best friend's wife—although I learn
that nowadays such occurrences are commonplace.'

Felicia's face flushed.

'Not in the circles in which I move,' she denied
energetically.

Raschid's eyebrows rose and he shrugged dismissively.
'It matters little to me one way or the other, so you may
save your protestations for other ears. Now, if you have
seen enough, I suggest we return to the car.'

'But I haven't bought Zahra a present,' Felicia began
in dismay, faltering into silence as Raschid turned to stare
at her.

'*That* was why you agreed to come? What did you have
in mind?'

He looked so bored and remote that Felicia amost
stamped her foot.

'It isn't what I have in mind, but what I can afford,'
she said bluntly, gesturing towards the jeweller's window.
'Certainly nothing in there.'

For a moment she thought she saw his mouth curl in
faint, amused condescension.

'No,' he agreed. 'Sadeer's is probably the most expensive jeweller's in Kuwait, and anyway, you could not

hope to rival the gifts Zahra will receive from Saud and her family.'

'It isn't a question of "rivalling",' Felicia stormed, furious at his lack of understanding. 'It would be embarrassing and impolite if I had no present for her.'

'Are you asking for my help?'

Was she? She fought against a desire to tell him to go to hell and instead nodded her head mutely.

Was that satisfaction she read in his smile? Seething, she stared across the road, not really seeing the constant stream of opulent cars flashing past.

'Very well, Mis Gordon.' He took her arm, guiding her across the road towards a narrow alley, but before they could enter it a young woman hailed them, her eyes heavily kohled and her jeans and thin cotton blouse a replica of the uniform worn by her Western sisters. Felicia judged her to be around her own age, perhaps a little younger, allowing for the fact that girls from the East matured more quickly. She had the impression that Raschid would have preferred not to acknowledge her, and yet his smile was polite enough, and he listened attentively enough while she talked in rapid Arabic.

'Yasmin is the daughter of a friend of mine,' he explained for her benefit, commanding the other girl to speak in English. 'She was at university in England for a while. Miss Gordon is a friend of Faisal's, Yasmin, and is staying with us for a while.'

'While Faisal is in New York?' She tossed her long, dark hair and eyed Felicia assessingly. 'I wonder if he knows how friendly you are with his "friend" Raschid, or perhaps he no longer minds sharing.'

She was gone before Felicia could say anything, and Raschid watched her depart in grim silence.

'If you found Yasmin's hostility strange, perhaps I should explain that she is one of the casualties of Faisal's ability to fall in and out of love. They became very close when she was in England, and I suspect she read more meaning into my description of you as Faisal's "friend" than I would have wished. No matter. . . . She is hardly likely to broadcast the true nature of your relationship. Not in view of her own feelings for Faisal.'

Yasmin and Faisal! Strange that the thought of them together caused her no jealousy, Felicia reflected. Indeed what she actually felt for the other girl was a vague pity, despite her insinuating remarks concerning herself and Raschid. 'Sharing' indeed! If only she knew! A bitter smile curved her mouth. She was the last woman Raschid would want in his life.

Raschid directed her down the narrow alleyway, shadowed and almost secret in the blank face it showed to the world.

Plainly he knew where he was going. He guided her through a labyrinth of narrow streets, some built from the original mud bricks from which the earlier town had been constructed.

'Where are you taking me?' she asked him at one point, alarmed by the sudden transformation from West to East, as cloaked figures shuffled silently past them, and exotic, unrecognisable fragrances filled the air.

Raschid chuckled.

'Not to the slave market, if that's what you think. Oh yes, they still have them in the more remote oases, where captured tribes are sold as slaves. It is illegal, of course,' he shrugged, 'but by the time the crime is discovered it is often too late to prevent it. All that one can do is to make sure that the unfortunate victims are set free.'

Felicia shuddered, suddenly glad of his tall presence at her side. They were walking through an old-fashioned covered *souk*, where merchants called to passers-by from their open doorways. Above one hung jewelled Eastern rugs so beautiful that Felicia stopped to stare.

'They are made by Badu from Iran,' Raschid told her. 'They use patterns passed down from generation to generation.'

The merchant called out a greeting, sensing a possible

sale, but although Raschid acknowledged his presence, he did not stop.

Eventually he touched Felicia lightly on the arm, directing her footsteps towards an open doorway.

When her eyes had accustomed themselves to the darkness within the small shop Felicia saw that the shelves were stacked with bottles and boxes, the air redolent with cedarwood, ambergris, sandalwood, and other scents too unfamiliar for her to recognise. With dawning delight she realised that Raschid had brought her to the shop of a maker of perfumes.

While she stared round her surroundings in an absorbed trance the two men talked in low undertones. The owner of the shop was as wizened as a walnut, his face dried and seamed by time, but the dark eyes that glanced at Felicia were shrewdly assessing. He said something to Raschid and Felicia saw him shake his head, his expression cold.

'Will he be able to mix something for Zahra without seeing her?' Felicia whispered anxiously, wondering what they had been saying.

'The perfume is for Sitt Zahra?' the old man asked, betraying a knowledge of English Felicia would not have expected. Under her fascinated gaze the old man ran his eyes along the shelves, at last removing one small bottle. 'I have here the perfume I made for her the last time she came. If the Sitt cares to purchase some?'

It was dark in the interior of the shop, but Felicia saw Raschid nod his head, as she glanced at him for guidance.

'Yes, please,' she murmured.

A wide grin split the merchant's face.

'May Allah curse me, I had almost forgotten that the Sitt is to be married shortly. We must add something for fertility, and something else to enhance the womanhood that will shortly be hers.'

While they waited he measured and poured, sniffing occasionally, and then he was transferring the mixture to a small crystal jar.

'May I smell it?' Felicia asked eagerly.

To her disappointment he shook his head.

'This perfume is not harmonious to the Sitt's beauty.' He turned to Raschid and said something in Arabic, before saying to Felicia, 'Your beauty is that of the rose before it opens fully; a bud which has not yet blossomed, and so it must be with your perfume.'

Felicia was glad of the darkness to hide her blushes, as he handed the small package to her. She dared not look at Raschid, fearful of what she might see in his face. And yet the old man had been uncannily correct; she was still a 'bud', the petals of innocence furled tightly about her, awaiting the warmth of a man's lovemaking, before she could blossom into full flower.

In silence she followed Raschid from the shop, dazzled by the bright glare of the sun. It was the hour when the shops closed for the afternoon and everywhere shutters were being placed over windows, and doors closed against the heat. They were just emerging into the street when the perfume blender called something after them, and Raschid turned, glancing back into the scented darkness they had just left.

'One moment,' he said curtly, and disappeared back inside.

Felicia hesitated, unsure whether or not she ought to follow him. The two men were deep in a low-toned conversation, and unwilling to appear curious, she hovered in the doorway.

The old Arab was busily searching his shelves, moving jars and bottles. She caught the elusive scent of English lavender, instantly evocative of home, and then a more subtle, spicy scent. The old man pounded something in a wooden bowl with a small pestle and the fragrance of wild violets drenched the air. Fascinated, Felicia watched. Raschid was buying more perfume? For his sister? Then why the low-toned conversation? Some other woman, perhaps? A sophisticated creature with the chameleon ability to make the transition from East to West?

A woman who would guard her beauty from curious eyes in public but who had the self-confidence to reveal it without shyness to the man she loved—in private?

'Miss Gordon?'

How many more times would she have to endure hearing her name called in those bitingly imperious tones?

Her errant footsteps had taken her beyond the confines of the shop and cool exasperation laced Raschid's voice as he strode towards her.

'Has all that my sister and I have said to you been as so many grains of sand dispersed by the winds, or is it merely wilful caprice that prompts you into such constant disobedience?'

Disobedience! Felicia spun round, her eyes darkened to jade green with anger. Dear God, she did not want to quarrel with this man, but neither would she let him walk roughshod over her pride, trampling it beneath the fiery scorn of his contempt.

'I walked away because I didn't want to intrude,' she flung at him. 'Your business was plainly private.' Anger made her reckless. 'A gift for some woman who is permitted to share your bed, but forbidden any other part in your life. . . .'

'You have described the *type* of person for whom the perfume was intended to a nicety,' Raschid gritted at her. 'But the perfume maker does not share my view of you, Miss Gordon. Oh yes!' He laughed scornfully at her shocked expression. 'Did you not guess? The old man was making the perfume for you—his own idea, not mine, I hasten to add. Here, take it,' he commanded, thrusting a small package into her hand. 'He insists that it incorporates the innocence which he claims is an integral part of your nature. I did not want to tell him that his eyesight must be failing if that is what he thinks. I know my nephew, Miss Gordon,' he concluded grimly, 'and I know the type of women who share his life.'

Felicia turned, intent only on escaping from his cruel

words, but his hands reached out and stayed her, his expression cautionary.

'Do not be foolish,' he advised her. 'Even nowadays the souks are not entirely free from danger for the unwary. Your careless footsteps might have led you down any one of a hundred alleys and before too long you would have been hopelessly lost—an experience I am sure neither of us wishes to endure.'

She pictured herself, lost and frightened, dependent on this cold, autocratic man for succour, and her chin lifted proudly.

'You need not worry, Sheikh Raschid,' she told him. 'If I were lost, *you* would be the last man I would want to rescue me.'

She pulled away from him as she spoke and a piece of flint half buried in the sun-baked earth caught her unprotected ankle, lacerating the soft skin. She winced as pain shot through her and blood welled from the cut.

Raschid tensed, frowning as he heard her involuntary protest, then dropped on to his haunches, a muttered curse falling softly into the golden silence of the afternoon when he saw what had happened.

'It's nothing,' Felicia protested unsteadily as lean fingers probed the wound with surprising gentleness.

'It's bleeding. It must be washed and cleaned,' Raschid replied curtly.

There were some moistened tissues in her bag which she used to keep her hands and face fresh and she opened it, removing them.

'I'll do that.'

The authoritative tone could not be ignored, and in silence she handed Raschid the moistened pad, flinching a little at its coolness against her throbbing flesh.

'How one admires the British in adversity,' Raschid mocked as he straightened up. 'So cool, so controlled . . . so prepared for every contingency.'

The light in his eyes reminded her that a few nights ago there had been a contingency for which she had not been prepared, but Felicia ignored it, murmuring lightly, 'One tries. . . .'

'Indeed one does. But sometimes we must fail, for the good of our souls.'

Was he warning her that she would fail to convince him to allow her marriage to Faisal? She moved away, wincing afresh as she put her full weight on her ankle. Raschid's hand on her wrist steadied her; a momentary contact—no more—but in that moment the air between them seemed fraught with some intangible emotion and then she was free, the clean male scent of him fading from her nostrils as quickly as the imprint of his fingers was fading from her wrist.

'What's the matter?'

Her eyelashes flicked down, but not in time to prevent him from reading the expression in her eyes. He laughed softly.

'Ah yes, I see! You thought perhaps I might repeat our romantic scene of the other night. I'm afraid I must disappoint you, Miss Gordon.'

'Romantic? Is that what you call it?' Felicia retorted bitterly. 'Then you have very strange ideas of romance, Sheikh.' She turned away, anger and resentment flaring simultaneously to heated life, possessed by an urge to escape from this man and his tormenting mockery; a desire to put as much distance between them as possible, heedless of the dangers.

In the empty *souk* her heartbeat thundered in her ears, steadily increasing as she hurried past shuttered shop fronts, like so many unseeing eyes, disdainful of the folly of the pale foreigner who ran unveiled along the shadowed alley. Pain throbbed through her ankle, but she disregarded it. The thudding of her heart drowned out every other sound bar one—the relentless footsteps behind her, firm and tireless, driving her like a terrified gazelle before the beaters.

He caught her, as she had known he must, his fingers biting into her waist as he swung her back against him, shaking her until she thought her neck must break.

'You little fool! Don't you know any better than to run in this heat? Do you really want me to give you a reason to run from me?'

Felicia looked up at the thin line of his mouth, harshly forbidding, and a tremor of something so alien and unwanted shot through her that at first she did not recognise it. When she did the shock was so great that she could barely comprehend that *she*, a girl who had never deliberately set out to arouse any man, and indeed shrank from physical contact, had felt a thrill of surging satisfaction at the blazing anger in Raschid's eyes, and a desire to push him over the limits of his control, her own fury fuelled by his.

Common sense warned her that the ensuing conflagration could destroy her totally, but she no longer cared. She wanted Raschid to experience anger as consuming as her own; to endure the lash of her contempt against his pride, as she had been forced to endure his.

'Well, Miss Gordon?'

'You have already given me sufficient reason, but in your arrogance you will not admit it.'

His fingers curled round the soft flesh of her upper arms, frightening in their intensity. He smiled without pity when she winced at their crushing pressure.

'This is the East,' he reminded her. 'I could punish you here and now for what you have just said and no man would raise his hand against me, not even if I beat you publicly in the streets. Beware! In every man there lurks the falcon; a streak of ruthlessness and thirst for power.'

His fingers lifted to her throat, trapping the wildly beating pulse she could no longer control. All at once the fight had gone out of her, and where there had been momentary elation there now was dread. He laughed mirthlessly when she shivered under his touch, nervous as the silky-maned Arab mares of the Badu.

'You see?' he taunted. 'At last you realise that a man is

not an equal, but an alien force, bent on destruction when he is aroused to anger.'

'Stop it! Stop it at once,' Felicia begged him. 'I won't listen to you!' Her voice trembled, caught somewhere between indignation and fear. 'You don't deceive me at all. You're hoping to drive me away; to frighten me into giving up Faisal. You think I'll be overpowered by that potent masculinity you're so proud of, like a timid, shrinking Victorian heroine, caught in the trap of her own senses. Well, you're going to be disappointed! I'm well aware of the difference between my senses and my heart.'

'Are you indeed?' he challenged softly, the sensuous movement of his thumb against the silkiness of her neck making her aware too late of her danger. She trembled under the deliberate provocation of the caress and he laughed, deep in his throat.

'And what do your senses tell you now, Miss Gordon?'

It was too late to pretend that his touch left her un-affected, too late by far to wish she had never allowed fury to betray her into this hopelessly untenable position. She closed her eyes and gritted bitterly:

'They tell me that sex without love is like the desert without water—an arid wasteland where nothing can flourish.'

'But that arid wasteland, as you call it, possesses a magic of its own.'

His thumb was stroking along her jaw now, the steel fingers forcing her chin to tilt upwards no matter how much she fought against their pressure. She opened her eyes. His were barely inches away, darkly grey, the sen-suously curving mouth smiling thinly.

He bent his head towards her, and she was like the falcon's prey, transfixed, accepting her fate. His faint breath stirred her hair.

'Have you experienced the potency of the desert, Miss Gordon?'

Dear God, what was happening to her? With an an-guished cry she tore herself free. What was he trying to do to her? Seduce her away from Faisal? Faisal! Why had she not thought of him before now? Why had the memory of his lovemaking not protected her from responding to Raschid?

Gathering the tattered remnants of her pride about her, she stared coldly at the man towering over her.

'The desert holds no attraction for me, Sheikh Raschid—and neither do you.'

CHAPTER SIX

TALK about the best laid plans of mice and men! Felicia
thought ruefully as she dressed for dinner. A cowardly
corner of her heart prayed that Raschid would be absent
from the meal. She stared critically in the mirror at her
too-pale face. She had known from the start that her self-
imposed task was hopeless, but after this afternoon she
could never hope to convince Raschid that she would
make Faisal a good wife. She shrugged bravely. What did
it matter, after all? He could hardly swear on the Bible that
there had been no provocation! Provocation! Colour
washed over her skin as she remembered the sensuous
movement of his thumb against her flesh, and the peculiar
weakness that had made her legs feel as though they had
turned to an unset jelly.

All sheer magnetism, of course. She wielded her hair-
brush fiercely for a few seconds until the auburn curls
framed her small face in a silky cloud. Raschid had done
it deliberately—there could be no doubt about that!
Playing on her fears and uncertainties, unleashing the
powerful aura of his masculinity. And how near she had
come to succumbing!

Slowly she put the brush down, staring at her trembling
mouth and wary eyes. There was the crux of the matter.
She had been dangerously affected by Raschid's caresses;
so much so that shame scorched her as she made herself
relive those seconds in her arms. She had deliberately
encouraged him to unleash his anger against her, but she
had never dreamed it would take such a damagingly sensuous course, or that she herself would be swept away in
its fierce tide. In vain she told herself that it was merely
an automatically feminine reaction, trying desperately to
drive away the tormenting image of Raschid's taunting

smile by replacing it with Faisal's loving smile. But for some reason she found it impossible to reconstruct his boyish features; the memory eluded her, as though over-powered by Raschid's stronger personality. The harder she tried to cling to the memory of Faisal, the more diffi-cult she found it to superimpose his features over Raschid's. Honesty had always been one of her strong points, and now she was forced to question the strength of her feelings.

Could there be a grain of truth in Raschid's accusation that her love for Faisal was founded on what he could give her—Oh, not wealth, that mattered little—but secu-rity, warmth, the affection and companionship of a family. The more she contemplated this point, the more plausible it became. Faisal had surrounded her in warmth and love, and she had sunk into its security without deeply ques-tioning her own feelings. It had been enough merely to be loved. But would it always be enough? And wasn't she cheating Faisal as surely as though she had merely wanted him for his money?

She was glad when the dinner gong put an end to these useless speculations. She was bound to have doubts, second thoughts, but once she and Faisal were together again. . . . . Not even in the tiniest corner of her heart was she willing to admit that her real doubts sprang from the untenable discovery that while Faisal's lovemaking affected her hardly at all physically, Raschid had merely to touch her to send her pulses racing, her body flooded with sexual awareness.

Dislike could be as powerful an emotion as love, she reminded herself, as she zipped up her dress and added a quick touch of lipstick to the soft curves of her mouth. It toned with the pink in her dress, swirls of pink and pale green chiffon, an unusual combination for a redhead, but one that brought an indefinable touch of the exotic to her appearance, darkening the colour of her eyes and high-lighting the richness of her hair. A lacy white stole covered her shoulders, although the dress had small cap sleeves and a neckline that was discretion itself. Untouched on the dressing table was the perfume Raschid had given her. She refused to open it; for a moment tempted to dispose of it in the same way as she had disposed of the glass paperweight, but acknowledging that the perfume had come from the perfume-maker and not Raschid. Even so she was reluctant to discover what sort of woman he had thought her, and she pushed the small package to the back of her drawer, unwilling for Zahra's curious eyes to alight on it.

She was the first downstairs, and on impulse she hurried into the gardens, to where she had thrown the blue leather box. It had been stupid to try to destroy a thing of so much beauty out of momentary pique, but although she searched diligently among the rose bushes she could find no trace of the package and surmised that the gardener must have disposed of it.

Tonight the delicious spicy aromas coming from the dining room did nothing to tempt her appetite. Her stomach muscles knotting with tension at the thought of having to face Raschid, she felt as though the merest morsel of food would choke her.

Zahra greeted her in her normal ebullient fashion, smiling approvingly at the cool picture Felicia made; the fresh green colours of an English spring flowering in the desert.

'Uncle Raschid will not be joining us tonight—he is entertaining business acquaintances,' Zahra explained as they sat down.

Felicia relaxed with relief. So at least one of her wishes had been granted. Now all she needed was for her good fairy to wave her wand twice more—once to bring Faisal home and a second time to dissipate Raschid's dislike—but such wishes were hardly likely to be granted, not if Raschid had anything to do with it.

'Did your sightseeing tire you?' Zahra asked solicitously. 'You look very pale.'

'A little.' But it wasn't her tour of the shops and town

that had left her feeling so drained, it was her clash with
Raschid and the disturbing thoughts it had aroused. Now
wasn't the time to question the strength of her feelings for
Faisal, but for some reason she was finding it increasingly
difficult not to compare Faisal to his uncle. Raschid would
never allow anyone to dictate his way of life! She was
being unfair, she reminded herself. Faisal had very little
choice in the matter. Raschid had the whip hand!

'Has Zahra told you that my elder daughter and her
family are to pay us a visit shortly?' Umm Faisal asked,
as Selina heaped Felicia's plate with savoury saffron rice.

Felicia shook her head and looked enquiringly at
Zahra.

'Yes, it is true,' the younger girl acknowledged. 'Nadia
is to join us at the oasis. You will like her, Felicia, she
looks very much like Faisal.' She smiled understandingly
when Felicia flushed; which only increased her own feelings of guilt, for it had been of Raschid's darkly sardonic
features of which she had been thinking and not Faisal's.

She toyed listlessly with her food while Umm Faisal
and Zahra discussed the arrangements which had to be
made for the trip to the oasis. Was the memory of this
afternoon's unpleasantness destroying Raschid's appetite?
Did a mental image of her face torment him? Somehow
she doubted it.

Refusing coffee, Felicia excused herself. Her small white
lie that she had a headache was not entirely untrue. The
beginnings of tension in the back of her neck had spread
to her temples and she was glad to lie down on her bed
and let her mind wander at will, relaxing under the hypnotic hum of the air-conditioning and the perfumed velvet
of the Eastern night.

A tap on the door roused her, and she sat up and smiled
reassuringly at Selina when she poked her head round the
door.

'The Sitt is wanted downstairs in Sheikh Raschid's
study.'

At first Felicia thought the girl had made a mistake,

and knowing that her English could not always be relied upon, she shook her head kindly. 'Sheikh Raschid is entertaining some friends, Selina, I do not think he would want me to join him.'

'Friends all gone,' Selina replied firmly. 'Sheikh alone now. Everything quite proper. If the Sitt will come.'

It was obvious that she intended to wait and escort her downstairs, Felicia realised in exasperation. Her dress was slightly creased where she had been lying on it, but there was no time to worry about that now, nor to drag a comb through her unruly curls and wish that tiredness did not give her face such a look of soft vulnerability.

What could Raschid want? A further reiteration of his disapproval? She hesitated, and Selina paused enquiringly at the bottom of the stairs. Giving herself a mental shake, Felicia followed. After all, what could Raschid do? Eat her?

Raschid's apartments were reached by a corridor linking them with the harem quarters of the house. They had their own private entrance and a large square hall furnished with soft Persian carpets and an intricately carved brassbound chest, plainly of great antiquity. Old-fashioned oil lamps threw a soft glow across the well polished floor.

There was richness here, and simplicity too, the one harmoniously blending with the other to give a feeling of timeless serenity which had the immediate effect of soothing her ragged nerves. The tall, narrow windows were open to the night, and the sharp scent of the lime trees stole in with the dusk.

'This is the Sheikh's study, *sitt*,' Selina said respectfully, motioning her towards an iron-studded wooden door. Felicia gave her a wan smile, uncertain as to whether she should go straight in or knock. The decision was made for her when the door opened abruptly.

In the half light Raschid seemed to tower above her, and Felicia bit back a gasp. She would never have recognised him. He was wearing a *dishdasha*—the traditional

white flowing robe of the Kuwaitis—his headdress hiding
the night-black hair, a dark cloak lavishly embroidered
with gold thread worn casually across his broad shoulders.

'What is the matter, Miss Gordon?' he asked urbanely
as he ushered her into the room.

'N-nothing,' Felicia stammered, but her eyes remained
glued to the undeniably impressive figure he made,
outlined against the starkness of the white walls.

'When dealing with my compatriots I find it better to
wear the traditional garb of our country. In point of fact
the *dishdasha* is more comfortable by far than Western-
style suits.'

'And far more impressive.' She could have bitten her
tongue out, when he turned and stared coolly at her. A
frisson of awareness tingled across her skin, and she
shivered slightly, despite the warmth of the night.

'And what, I wonder, does *that* remark imply? That
you think me a posturing fool, practising for a part in *The
Desert Song*?'

Anger underwrote the cold words. Horrified, Felicia
stammered a denial. No European could ever have worn
the flowing garment with the grace of his Arab counter-
part, and her surprise had sprung merely from the fact
that this was the first time she had seen Raschid dressed
in the traditional manner. Although she would not have
admitted it to a soul, when he opened the door to her, for
a moment he had embodied every single one of her
romantic teenage dreams.

And now to crown all her other follies she had offended
Raschid's pride, touching the most sensitive spot of his
personality. She bit her lip, wishing they were on good
enough terms for her to explain that he had misunderstood.

'What? Nothing to say for yourself?' he asked harshly,
surprising her with the raw anger she sensed beneath the
words. He moved with the stealth of the desert fox and
the sureness of an Arab stallion, coming to stand at her

side and spinning her round to face him.

Felicia moistened her lips, wetting them with a nervous tongue, the movement instantly stilled as Raschid's gaze pounced on the betraying gesture.

'Why did you send for me?'

He released her, and she could feel her nerve ends quivering with relief as the tension eased.

'Merely to give you this,' he replied, handing her an envelope bearing an airmail stamp.

Her heart lurched. It was from Faisal; it must be! With eager fingers she reached for the envelope, and her hand brushed against Raschid's as she did so. It was like receiving an electric shock. She shrank back, recoiling from the contact, her face pale as she gripped her letter.

'You may cease the charade, Miss Gordon,' Raschid mocked. 'The ordeal is over. You have your letter, which you can take to your lonely bed to read and perhaps remember the nights you have spent in my nephew's arms. Faisal is no stranger to the delights of the flesh, but then I have no need to remind you of that, have I?'

'No, you have not,' Felicia agreed, suppressing her instinctive denial of his accusations. For some reason allowing Raschid to believe that she and Faisal were lovers made her feel safer, although why she could not have said.

She saw his face darken, tightening with anger and contempt. No doubt she had just confirmed his initial impression of her, but she no longer cared. Secretly in the hidden recesses of her heart she was beginning to doubt her own ability to make Faisal happy, but her pride would not allow her to admit her discovery to Raschid. Time enough to know that he had been right when she was safely back in England, away from those mocking grey eyes.

By the time she reached her room she was trembling with a mixture of anger and pain. Feverishly she ripped open Faisal's envelope, withdrawing the letter with a fast-beating heart. Surely here she would find the reassurance

that she so badly needed? Surely the written words of
Faisal's love for her would banish all her doubts?

The letter was depressingly short, barely more than a
few scrawled lines, with none of the tender reassurances
she had hoped for. Indeed, it struck Felicia, as she read
the letter for a second time, that Faisal too might be
having second thoughts. He had written more as though
to a friend than a lover; the phrases stilted and cautious;
one betraying sentence almost leaping off the paper.

'.... New York is much more fun than I had
imagined. . . .'

With a sinking heart Felicia remembered what Raschid
had told her about Faisal's propensity for falling in and
out of love. At the time she had thought he was merely
trying to upset her, but now she was not so sure. Faisal's
letter was not that of a man deeply in love and committed
to that love. Now, when it was too late, Felicia wished
passionately that she had not allowed him to persuade
her to come to Kuwait, and worse still, to spend her hard-
earned savings. With a feeling of sick despair she acknowledged that had it been possible she would have gone
straight to the airport first thing in the morning and
booked her flight home.

She even toyed with the idea of contacting her aunt
and requesting her help with the fare, but she knew she
could not. It seemed ironical that the one person who
would have been more than glad to finance her return to
England was the one man in the world she would never
ask.

No, distasteful though it was, she would have to write
to Faisal and sort things out. Once he knew that she was
no longer expecting to become his wife, he would probably
be delighted to pay for her ticket, she thought wryly.

As she switched off the lamp and slid down between
the cool sheets, she wondered morosely why the discovery
that Faisal no longer loved her should affect her so little.
Less than a week ago he had formed her entire world;
now all she wanted was to return home. And yet she

would miss this land, she admitted. Despite its alienness it had touched her heart, and she felt that she could have adapted had her love for Faisal been strong enough.

Her last thought before sleep claimed her was that at least she was having a small measure of revenge against Raschid. While she slept in the knowledge that she and Faisal would never marry, Raschid was probably lying awake thinking of ways to part them. Strangely enough the thought brought her precious little comfort.

Although she felt no guilt at deceiving Raschid, it was far harder having to pretend with Zahra. She would have liked to have the younger girl as a sister-in-law, she acknowledged, as Zahra waylaid her on the way to breakfast, bouncing up and down in excitement.

'Look what Raschid has given me as a pre-birthday present!' she exclaimed, waving a cheque in front of Felicia's bemused eyes, and gloating gleefully over its size, enlarging enthusiastically on how she intended to spend it.

'There's a shop in Kuwait that sells the most dreamy lingerie!' She rolled her eyes dramatically. 'How about coming with me this afternoon?'

Felicia hadn't the heart to refuse her, and Zahra's grateful hug when she nodded her head was more than reward enough.

Ali drove them into Kuwait, dropping them in the area of Fahd Salim Street, where Raschid had taken her the day before.

As Felicia had half expected, Zahra tended to linger over the glittering displays of jewellery.

'Those pearls come from the gulf,' she told an interested Felicia. 'Until oil was discovered, pearls were Kuwait's richest source of income.'

Ali hovered protectively behind them, reminding them that they had not come to window-gaze. As before, Felicia was impressed by the graceful boulevard with its trees and flowers.

'Our government is spending a great deal of money on irrigation schemes and desalination plants,' Zahra told her. 'In the fruit markets you will find all manner of fruits and vegetables grown on specially developed farms. The sun, once our greatest enemy, is being harnessed to provide the energy to grow perpetual crops. Saud is studying agriculture at the university,' she added by way of an explanation for all her knowledge. 'His family own lands near to our own at the oasis and he and Raschid are hoping to develop a fruit farm there eventually.' She pulled a wry face. 'I'm not sure what he loves best—me, or his precious greenhouses.' She touched Felicia's arm, motioning towards one of the shops. 'In here. Ali will wait outside for us.'

The shop was small—no more than a boutique really— the walls hung with pale green silk panels, tiny gilt chairs covered in the same fabric, standing on an off-white deep-pile carpet. No pretensions to Eastern origins here; the boutique was blatantly Bond Street, or Fifth Avenue.

A mouthwatering selection of satin and lace underwear was produced for Zahra's inspection, and as she fingered a peach satin nightdress lavishly trimmed with coffee lace, Felicia reflected rather enviously on the advantages of possessing a wealthy and generous uncle. Not that she would want Raschid to pay for her trousseau. The thought made her go hot and cold, and the peach satin dropped from her fingers as though it had burned.

'Something wrong?'

'What? Oh no—nothing. I think you should have the peach, Zahra, and the pale blue nightdress and negligee set.'

'What about this one?'

Felicia examined the nightdress she was holding up for her inspection. It was a filmy mist of sea-green shifting to jade, in a silken shimmer of the finest gossamer chiffon.

'It's lovely,' Felicia admitted.

'And most suitable for a bride,' the sales assistant pressed.

'Would you not like something like this for your own marriage?' Zahra asked, much to Felicia's embarrassment. She closed her mind to a vision of herself clad only in the whispering chiffon, held in the arms of . . . Not Faisal, that was for sure, she told herself, shaking her head and handing the nightgown back to Zahra.

Ali was still waiting patiently outside, and something about the set of his shoulders suggested that they had been gone rather a long time.

'Anything else you want?' she asked Zahra, and the other girl shook her head.

They were crossing the wide pavement when Felicia saw the familiar figure striding towards them, and her heart gave a double somersault before hammering urgently against her ribs.

'Isn't that Raschid?' she asked Zahra, surprised when the younger girl compressed her lips and immediately turned in the opposite direction.

'What's the matter?'

'Didn't you see that woman with him?' Zahra hissed.

Felicia had. The woman was tall and dark, dressed with an understated elegance, wrapped in an aura of wealth. Felicia had guessed her age to be somewhere in her late twenties.

'She must be his mistress,' Zahra decided. 'She cannot be a woman of good family, otherwise she would never walk openly in the street with him.'

So Raschid had a mistress! Why should Felicia feel so surprised? She already knew how potently male he was; surely it should not be surprising that there were other women in his life besides his sister and niece. So why had her legs suddenly turned to quivering jelly; the muscles in her stomach cramping in agonised protest? The hypocritical pig! Resentment fanned the flames of her anger. How dared he insult and revile *her*, when she was quite innocent of all his accusations, and yet openly flaunt his mistress through the streets!

Suddenly she longed to confront him; to sneer con-

temptuously at him as he had done at her, and when she
hesitated, Zahra grabbed her hand, shaking her head.

'It would embarrass Raschid if he saw us. He could not
acknowledge us while he is with *her*!'

Embarrassed? Raschid?

Zahra, correctly interpreting her expression, added seriously, 'He *would* be embarrassed, as I would myself.
Naturally a single man has certain . . . needs, but . . . .' She
shrugged comprehensively, trying to convey the impossibility of introducing the women who served those
'needs' to the sheltered females of his own family. Felicia
stared unseeingly ahead. Was that how Raschid thought
of her? As the woman who served the 'needs' of his
nephew? Shame and rage scorched her, and her fingers
balled into two small fists.

'What's wrong?' Zahra asked. 'You look so fierce.'

'Oh, it's nothing.' But she knew she was lying. A queer
little pain had lodged somewhere in the region of her
heart, but she steadfastly ignored it. Why should she care
if Raschid chose to walk side by side with some dusky
beauty, his dark head inclined towards her in a gesture of
attentive protection? She had no need of his protection,
nor his attention. How could she, when all that existed
between them was open dislike?

Naturally on their return to the villa Zahra had to inspect
her purchases all over again, although Felicia was surprised when she did not unwrap the sea-green chiffon.
Perhaps she was frightened of soiling it, she decided.
Together they enthused over the peach satin, as Felicia
held it against Zahra's skin.

'I doubt your Saud will have eyes to spare for anything
but you,' she teased. 'Which one will you wear on your
wedding night?'

'Neither,' Zahra replied seriously. 'Our wedding will
be completely traditional. It is my wish and Saud's. I
shall be dressed in my bridal caftan with its one hundred
and one buttons down the front, and round my neck will

be the gold necklaces given to me by my family and Saud's.' When Felicia still looked puzzled, she explained, 'It is our custom for the bridegroom to remove the necklaces one by one while the bride keeps a modest silence. Then he unfastens the buttons, starting at the hem,' she blushed a little. 'You find it strange, perhaps, that I should want to be married in this way, but . . .'

'No stranger than the wearing of a white dress in the West,' Felicia assured her. In point of fact a small lump had lodged in her throat, but the image shimmering in her mind was neither that of Zahra nor Faisal, but another dark, masculine head bent painstakingly over the tiny buttons, lean fingers making nonsense of their many fastenings. A deep shudder trembled through her, and her stomach churned with disturbing sensations. Dear God, what was she thinking? Imagining Raschid of all people kneeling tenderly at his bride's feet, his normally sardonic expression replaced by one of intimate desire. What was happening to her? She felt sick and dizzy, and had to sink down into a chair to try and gather her composure. If only she could go home. If only she had discovered that gratitude was not and never could be love, before she had come to Kuwait. If she had not left England she would never have discovered that it was possible to respond to the potent maleness of a man without even liking him; that one could be aware of everything about him, and yet still know nothing. Her mouth had gone dry, the strange ache in her heart seemed to grow with every breath she took.

'Did Faisal tell you when he would be coming home?' Zahra asked innocently. 'Last year he flew back from London just to give me my birthday present. Raschid arranged it.' Her face brightened. 'Perhaps he will do the same thing this year.'

Felicia shook her head. There was no point in raising the younger girl's hopes.

'I don't think so.'

'Raschid might do something if you went to him and

told him how much you are missing Faisal. Why don't you, Felicia? You must be longing to see him.'

She was. But not for the reasons that Zahra supposed. If Faisal were to return she could ask him to help her get home, but of course she could not say this to Zahra. Thank goodness she had not allowed him to persuade her into wearing the ring he had bought her.

'I'm sure you could coax Raschid round,' Zahra continued. 'He isn't a complete monster, you know.'

'That wasn't the impression I got this afternoon,' Felicia reminded her drily, remembering the younger girl's desire not to be seen.

'That was different,' Zahra replied promptly. 'Mother worries because Raschid does not marry. The responsibility of caring for her and us has aged him, I think, although he never lets us see it. Perhaps when I am married he will look for a wife, although it will not be easy. Mother fears that his English blood makes him impatient of our own girls.' She glanced speculatively at Felicia. 'Faisal must have told you how like Raschid's grandmother you are. I wouldn't have put it past him to have deliberately sent you out here to tease Raschid. When we were little I remember our father saying that Raschid, as a child, had been fascinated by the portrait of his grandmother. I think he has a softness for you, Felicia, even though he hides it.'

A softness for her! Felicia nearly told her how wrong she was, and why. So Zahra thought that Faisal's motives in sending her to Kuwait might not have been entirely altruistic. Felicia suspected that she might be right. It was obvious to her that there had been differences of opinion between Faisal and Raschid in the past, and she wondered if Faisal had announced their 'engagement' to Raschid, in a deliberate attempt to annoy him. It was not pleasant to realise that she might have been used in this fashion, and she was coming to accept that Faisal was not the charming young man he had seemed on the surface.

Once again Raschid did not join them for dinner, and when Umm Faisal explained that he was dining with friends, Felicia smiled rather mirthlessly to herself. Friends, or friend, in the singular? She was tired, and excused herself, going to her room.

Each day the temperature seemed to rise a little more and Felicia had grown quite used to rising each morning to a cloudless blue sky; the muezzin no longer a weirdly unfamiliar sound, but part and parcel of everyday life. She was coming to love this country of stark contrasts, she admitted, and would miss it when she left. She had still not written to Faisal, and she knew that it was a task she must complete, but her pride shrank from having to beg his aid. Sensitive to the opinions of others, she was reluctant to have him think that she expected him to pay her fare home. And yet what alternative did she have?

The scent of the roses reached her from her bedroom window. Throwing a crocheted shawl round her shoulders, she went downstairs, through the silent hall and into the welcome coolness of the garden. They were particularly attractive, these enclosed courtyards with their fountains and shady trees. The sharp, acid scent of the limes mingled with the fragrance of the roses. Doves cooed softly from the dovecote by the fountain. She trailed her fingers in the water, watching the fish slide quickly away. With the moon full the garden was almost as bright as day, the landscape etched in stark silver and black.

She sighed and froze as feet crunched on the gravel.

'Wishing there was someone to share the enchantment of our evenings with you, Miss Gordon?'

Raschid! Her hand crept to her throat to still the small pulse beating frantically there. He was dressed Arab fashion once more, one leather-booted foot resting arrogantly on the rim of the pool as he surveyed her. She bit back a sharp retort, swallowing her dismay.

'As a matter of fact I was,' she lied lightly, her hands clenching impotently at her sides, as his cool glance slid over her small, flushed face, resting momentarily on the rise and fall of her breasts beneath their thin covering, before lingering thoughtfully on her neat waist and the narrow tautness of her hips. For some reason it had become desperately important to conceal from Raschid the truth about her feelings for Faisal.

His eyebrows rose, and again she bit back the burning anger clamouring for utterance. All her senses were urging her to escape, but she would not let him see her fear.

'I believe you wish me to arrange for Faisal to come home? Zahra has been soliciting my forbearance on your behalf. Her tender heart aches for what she imagines to be the tragic parting of two star-crossed lovers. Naturally I have had to disabuse her of what is merely romantic fantasy.'

Forgetting her own doubts about her feelings for Faisal, she stared at him, her eyes blazing.

'By doing what? Giving her your interpretation of our relationship?'

'Oh, come,' he mocked mildly, 'why all the maidenly indignation? You made no demur the other night when I implied that you and Faisal had already shared the delights which Zahra only merely anticipates. You forget that I have lived in your country. I know in what scant regard your women hold their modesty and innocence.'

'Which, of course, a woman of your race would never do!'

'And what is that supposed to mean? Or can I guess? If you are referring to my companion of this afternoon—oh yes, I know you saw me, that hair of yours is instantly recognisable—she makes no pretence to being anything she is not.'

Felicia's lip curled in a fair imitation of his own sneer. 'Unlike you! I must admit that you surprised me. You don't look the type of man who needs to buy a woman's favours, but I suppose when all you can offer is physical gratification, the pill has to be sweetened somehow.'

His incredulous, 'Why, you little . . .' told her that she had managed to slip under his guard, but allied to trem-

bling satisfaction was the certainty that she would be
made to pay for that moment of victory.

Retribution came sooner than she had imagined.

'I sought you out because Zahra was concerned for you.
She tells me that you grow pale and do not eat, and she
attributes this to the fact that you are missing Faisal. I
know otherwise, but I will not be deceived by your play-
acting. I shall not allow Faisal to return now to be
ensnared by you all over again. However, we cannot have
you pining for lack of his lovemaking,' he told her silkily.
'It is fortunate that Zahra's window does not overlook
this courtyard—she may not approve of the methods I
employ to assuage your need of him.'

Zahra wasn't the only one who did not approve, Felicia
thought numbly as her flaying hands were captured and
pinned to her sides, as hard masculine lips plundered
the trembling softness of her own, parted to voice her
fury. She was forced backwards, imprisoned against
Raschid's arm, her throat and the swelling softness of her
breasts exposed to his merciless scrutiny. His eyes glittered
over the answering fury in her own, fastening on the erratic pulse beating frantically in her creamy throat before
lingering on the pale blur of flesh revealed by the V neckline of her cotton dress.

'Let me go!' she muttered furiously, her mouth throbbing, 'Save your kisses for the women who are obliged
to endure them in return for some worthless trinket!'

She heard the angry hiss of his escaping breath, hard
fingers tightened on her wrists, and her flesh burned from
the contact with his.

'Never worthless, Miss Gordon. I can assure you of
that.'

But despite the lazy drawl she knew that his anger was
no longer held in check. She had unleashed it with her
hasty words. She closed her eyes, against a sudden weak
rush of tears, as his hands moulded her hip bones, forcing
her against him. She would not cry now! She bit her lip.
She could feel the warmth of his breath against her face,

and stiffened, willing him to release her.

'Oh no, Miss Gordon, you will not escape so lightly this time!'

She could feel the tensile strength of his chest muscles against her breasts; the faintly harsh rasp of the dark hairs exposed by the open neck of his robe, so compellingly masculine that reaction flooded through her on a shock wave, making her painfully aware of just how inexperienced she actually was. The contact—which obviously meant nothing to him—suffocated her with its implied intimacy of flesh against flesh, and she struggled to get away, panicking as his lips took their fill of the exposed column of her throat, lingering appreciatively against her skin. If she had once doubted his skill and experience she could do so no longer. The deliberately arousing caresses would have melted ice; but she struggled not to give in; not to admit the drugging sensation of rising desire as his assault of her senses was subtly increased.

There was no affection or tenderness in his touch—she knew that; she knew that all he offered was the hollow sham of sexual need, and that even that was probably counterfeit, but she could do nothing when his free hand slid downward from her shoulder, cupping her breast, and stroking the soft curves.

Fear and indignation shot through her. Not even Faisal had touched her so intimately—nor so insultingly as though her body held no secrets, no pleasures, but merely the familiarity of the oft-known. She shuddered as his fingers found her nipple, coaxing it into hardening desire without exhibiting either haste or urgency; the pain and shock of her body's betrayal there for him to see in the widening of her eyes and tensed muscles.

Satisfaction gleamed in the night-dark eyes, as they raked her pale, shocked face.

'Well, now you can join the ranks of those who have known my objectionable touch, Miss Gordon. Although unlike them your reward was not well earned,' he taunted.

She reeled as he released her, hating the grim comprehension in his voice. There was a parcel in his hand, wrapped in tissue paper, and tied with green ribbon.

'It seems that Zahra purchased a gift for you on my behalf this afternoon. I only trust you will think of me when you wear it.'

The package was flung at her feet. Speech would have been a complete impossibility, as she stared up at him with hate-filled eyes.

'Pick it up,' he commanded inexorably. 'Otherwise I shall be obliged to deliver it again—in person, and since the gift has been given twice, it will have to be paid for twice.'

'You're nothing but a barbarian!' Felicia choked. 'I was a fool to think you could ever understand what I feel for Faisal . . . or any other *human* emotion!'

But mindful of the result of incurring his anger, she bent down and picked up the parcel, hating him with a bitterness that burned like vitriol.

'Do you know, Miss Gordon, this is by far the most pleasant sight I have had of you since you arrived— kneeling at my feet!'

She could not endure his goading. Not after what he had just forced upon her. Her voice shook with rage.

'Kneel before you? I'd as soon bow down to the Devil!'

She fled before he could retaliate, clutching the tissue paper in trembling fingers. In her room she flung it against the wardrobe door, and the fragile paper tore on the sharp edge of the handle, releasing a froth of sea-green chiffon.

She paled, staring at the silky fabric. The nightgown! Zahra had bought it for her! With Raschid's money! She was shivering with reaction and despair. In the mirror she could see the redness on her lips from his kisses. Her neck and shoulder burned from the searing heat of Raschid's practised kisses and her breast was on fire from the arrogant sureness of his hard caress. Her body stiffened with rage.

How dared he treat her like a woman he had bought for the night! She suppressed a wild sob. He had tainted her—stamped on her pride and destroyed the protective shield she had thrown around herself. Never again could she assert that desire was nothing without love and that she could never experience the former without the latter, because for one fleeting moment she *had* known desire; and it was that more than anything else that caused the hot tears to roll down her cheeks as her fingers curled furiously into her palms and she found some slight surcease in contemplating Raschid's muscular body writhing in mortal agony.

As for the nightdress. . . . She stared disparagingly at the fragile silk she had coveted not so many hours ago. She would burn it before she allowed it to come anywhere near her body!

CHAPTER SEVEN

BEMUSED, Felicia asked herself how on earth order would ever result from such chaos. The household was preparing to move to the oasis, and Zahra, lifting yet another armful of dresses from her wardrobe, said impishly that it was no wonder that Raschid had absented himself from the house. His excuse had been that he would go on before them to make sure that everything was in readiness for their arrival, but Felicia believed that if he had the smallest spark of decency he would be as anxious to avoid her company as she was his.

Never, if she lived to be a hundred, would she forget the emotionless destruction of her flimsy barriers, the calculated assault on her senses, and the bitter lessons she had learned. When she slept at night she dreamed of him, of his cold, jeering face, and most of all of his knowledgeable, caressing hands, and she would wake, trembling with anguish, tears cascading down her cheeks.

It was no wonder that she was losing weight. Several times she had started to pen a letter to Faisal, telling him as gently as she could that their love had died, but every time she reached the part where she had to beg him to send her the money for her fare home, her pride stopped her. She was reaching the point where she was contemplating paying a visit to the British Embassy, but Zahra's delight that she would be with them for her birthday celebrations prevented her from making a move until they returned from the oasis. She could manage for a few more days, she told herself, trying to believe that it was true.

'It's a pity that Raschid cannot spare Faisal,' Zahra mourned. A pity indeed, Felicia agreed, although she knew that the supposed 'emergency' that kept Faisal in New York was no more than a figment of Raschid's Machiavellian imagination.

She was helping Zahra with her packing. She had not imagined that a girl could possess so many clothes at the same time, and said as much.

Zahra grinned. 'Raschid makes me a very generous allowance.' She indicated a filmy harem outfit comprising baggy trousers in flame chiffon and a matching sequinned top. 'What do you think of that? I bought it for a joke. Raschid would be furious if he knew.' Felicia's raised eyebrows prompted a defensive outburst. 'Saud said it was a pity that harem dancers no longer existed, outside the imagination of Hollywood producers, and I thought. . . .'

'I can see what you thought,' Felicia murmured drily, amused and touched to see Zahra blushing a little. What business was it of Raschid's if the younger girl chose to play the harem dancer for her undoubtedly appreciative bridegroom? She folded the outfit briskly.

'It won't go in this box, it's full,' Zahra complained.

'Never mind, give it to me. I've plenty of room in my case.' Felicia looked rather quizzically at Zahra. 'Why do you want to take it? You won't be wearing it until you *are* married, I trust?'

'I daren't leave it here in case one of the maids sees it,' Zahra confessed. 'Mother wouldn't understand.'

'I can see why,' Felicia agreed, thinking of the transparent chiffon. It was obvious that Zahra was very much in love with her Saud, and Felicia wondered a little enviously what it was like to prepare for marriage basking in the warm approval of one's family. Had she ever anticipated Faisal's caresses with the enthusiasm with which Zahra looked forward to Saud's?—and not for the first time she questioned her ability to respond to a man's lovemaking. Had her uncle's cold rejection of her as a child destroyed her ability to give and receive love? And yet she *had* responded to Raschid. But she did not love him. She hated him. He was determined to destroy her, she thought bitterly, gathering up the small pile of garments which would not fit into Zahra's boxes and putting them in her own case. And he did not care what means he had to use to do so. She straightened up and her breast throbbed pulsatingly as it had done when he had touched her. Her face flaming, she squashed the impulse to place her own hand against her quickening flesh in an effort to eradicate the tingling memory.

It was not a great distance to the oasis when measured in mere miles, but the journey would take them through empty desert and careful preparations had to be made, checked and re-checked by Ali, who had been left in charge of their safety. Water bottles had to be filled, tires checked, and spare gasoline cans placed in the trunks of cars. They were to travel in convoy, the Mercedes carrying Umm Faisal, Zahra and Felicia, going first, three other cars with the staff and the luggage following on behind.

Felicia tended to be amused by the flurry of preparation, until Zahra pointed out the fate of other, less careful travellers. To die of thirst under a burning sun was no pleasant death, and could happen even to the most experienced desert traveller if a sandstorm blew up, obliterating the road, or a sharp stone pierced a gas tank, leaving them without transport.

It was just over a hundred miles to the oasis, but Felicia was ready to agree feelingly that it might have been a thousand, long before the green fringe of the palm trees warned her that journey's end was in sight. Even with the air-conditioning on full the heat inside the car was stifling, the sun dazzling as it bounced off the immaculate black hood of the Mercedes. The tires hissed wetly along the soft tarmac until they turned off on to a sandy track, throwing up clouds of fine dust to clog the throats and eyes of those driving behind.

'Now you see why we go first,' Zahra explained. 'The last vehicle is the most at risk. Even an expert driver can lose his way when the windscreen is covered in sand.'

Felicia repressed a small shudder at the thought of being lost in this vast wasteland. And yet for all its terrible emptiness the desert held a beauty all of its own. As far as the eye could see there was nothing but mile upon mile of never-ending sand, burning golden-red against the cobalt blue sky. The intensity of it hurt the eyes, and Felicia wondered anew at the tenacity of a people who had carved out their lives from this unyielding wilderness.

'Nearly there,' Zahra said cheerfully, as the fringe of palm trees on the horizon grew tantalisingly larger. 'You will love the oasis, Felicia. I believe Raschid considers it is our true home, although Faisal does not care for it in the same way, but in you I sense a sympathy for our ways. You do like our country, don't you?' she asked anxiously.

Felicia acknowledged that she had fallen under its spell, surprised to realise how true this was. Had circumstances been different, she would have been content to make her life in this magnificent, timeless land.

'Only one more day until Nadia arrives,' Zahra added. 'I'm longing to see her!'

Felicia hoped that Faisal's elder sister was as easy to get along with as his younger. Since the arrival of Faisal's letter she was conscious of being something of an impostor, in her own mind at least, and having Raschid as her enemy was more than enough to cope with.

It was dusk when they drove into the oasis, so Felicia could see very little of her surroundings apart from the clustering tops of palm trees, swaying lightly in the evening breeze, and the silky shine of moonlight on water as they drove past the silent oasis.

'Once the Badu camped here,' Zahra said softly, 'but now the tribesmen have retreated into the interior of the desert to pursue their chosen way of life unhindered.'

The house bore no resemblance to the villa outside Kuwait. Built of white stone, its narrow Moorish windows presented a blank face to the world. They drove through a fretted archway into a courtyard slightly similar to the one belonging to the villa, but whereas that was of modern construction combining the best of East and West, this one bore mute evidence of age. Behind them enormous iron-studded oak doors slammed shut, a reminder that once visitors to the oasis might not have been friendly. The soft-footed Moslem servants added to the sensation of having stepped back in time, and Felicia would not have been surprised to see a couple of Zahra's harem dancers wandering in the garden, the bracelets on their ankles tinkling in time to their sinuous movements.

Instead Ali ushered them into a large hallway, and then Felicia did gasp with amazed delight. Huge pillars of malachite supported an intricately patterned ceiling, painted in jewel-bright colours. She could hear the sound of water somewhere in the distance and the timeless enchantment of the East engulfed her.

Zahra laughed at her open-mouthed wonder.

'I knew you would like it!'

Ali and the other servants were bringing in their luggage, stacking it on the cool marble floor. Selina hurried away, promising that soon they would have a cup of coffee, and as the double doors at the other end of the hall opened, Felicia saw Raschid framed there, his flowing white robe in stark contrast to the rich bronze of his skin and the jewelled silks of the furnishings.

'Zahra will take you to the women's quarters, Miss Gordon. They overlook an inner courtyard. In the desert a wise man kept his rarest treasures under lock and key, and in my grandfather's day the women of the harem were never allowed outside the confines of this house. For my grandmother's pleasure he had a garden constructed inside the protective walls of his home so that she might enjoy the cool breeze that blows over the desert when dusk falls. She used to say that it reminded her of England.'

'You will love it, Felicia,' Zahra said softly, 'and the harem quarters. They are ridiculously exotic. Believe it or not, there is even a marble bath large enough to swim in.'

She laughed delightedly when Felicia flushed, exclaiming suddenly, 'Uncle Raschid, Felicia's eyes are exactly the same colour as these pillars!'

'The colour of malachite,' Raschid agreed, looking down at Felicia, and running his lean fingers caressingly down the pillar nearest to him. 'But I don't suppose Miss Gordon will be complimented to have her eyes compared with the cold hardness of marble—mm?'

As always his tone when he spoke to Zahra was teasingly indulgent, and Felicia was struck by the difference from when he addressed her.

Ali staggered in with more boxes, which he dropped by Felicia's cases. The top one fell on its side, bursting open to spill its contents in gay profusion across the floor. Felicia had been looking at Raschid and she saw his face change suddenly, from avuncular indulgence to grim disgust. He stepped forward, crossing the floor with a couple of lithe strides, bending to finger disdainfully the crimson chiffon billowing against the starkness of his robes.

Zahra trembled, casting Felicia a look of agonised appeal, and instantly she rose to the occasion. It didn't matter that Raschid's fingers were flicking the chiffon away with arrogant contempt, nor that his eyes were narrowing thoughtfully on her flushed face, his mouth curving downwards in contempt.

'Mine, I believe,' Felicia said bravely, with saccharine sweetness as she made a dive for the chiffon. Raschid was holding the fabric more firmly than she had realised and as she tugged ineffectually at it, the harem pants were revealed in their full glory. Almost she would have laughed at his distasteful expression as he relinquished the sequinned waistband after one look of incredulous contempt.

'I bought them in the *souk* the other day. I thought they might start a new fashion at home.' Some devil of mischief, too long submerged, suddenly reasserted itself prompting her to add flippantly, 'I hope Faisal likes them.' Demurely she let her eyelashes drop to veil her cheeks in mock modesty, even risking a coy giggle. 'They aren't the thing for shopping in Sainsbury's, of course, but for a quiet evening at home. . . .' She deliberately let her voice trail away, raising limpid eyes to the concentrated acidity in Raschid's and allowing just the merest hint of suggestiveness to peep through her assumed modesty. Watching his impassive features, she admitted that she was playing with fire, but shrugged the thought aside—in for a penny, in for a pound! When long seconds ticked by with Zahra frozen like a sphinx and Raschid's expression remotely unreadable she wondered if she had gone too far.

A cold grey glance, informed with deliberate and exactly calculated insult, roamed her body, oblivious to Zahra's shocked protest, and at length he drawled carelessly:

'Not your colour, I would have thought, Miss Gordon, with that hair.'

'No.' She was all smiling sweetness. 'You surprise me. I should have thought you would consider it *exactly* right for me, being scarlet.'

The way the heavy-lidded eyes narrowed told her that he had not missed the point, but he did not deign to answer and it was left to Ali to bundle up the rest of the clothes cascading across the floor and carry them from the room.

It was just as well that Raschid's annoyance with her was occupying the best part of his thoughts, Felicia reflected as she followed a thoroughly shaken Zahra, otherwise he might have realised that the rest of the clothes littering the floor had belonged not to her but to his niece!

It was a very subdued young girl who came into Felicia's room an hour later, when she was completing the last of her unpacking. The bedroom was as different from the one in Kuwait as chalk from cheese. For a start it was devoid of modern furnishings, apart from the comfortable double bed. The floor was polished wood, scattered with soft Persian rugs, of great age and value. A long low couch stuffed with cushions was set against one wall beneath the arched windows, tempting the languor-

ously inclined to relax and admire the cunning arrangement of trees and plants in the courtyard below. As in all
Arab houses of any wealth the sound of water was never
far away, for in days gone by an Arab could measure his
wealth in the amount of water he was able to waste.

A small dressing room had been fitted with wardrobes,
but it was on the ornamental brassbound chest that
Felicia had placed the carefully folded harem outfit.

Zahra pulled a face when she saw it.

'I've never seen Raschid so angry,' she said in a low
voice, her eyes disturbed. 'Oh, Felicia, I'm so sorry—the
way he looked at you—the things he said!'

'Well, now you know why I didn't enthuse over them
in the first place. But there's no harm done,' Felicia
assured her lightly.

'No harm!' Zahra's eyes filled with indignant tears.
'You can say that after the way Raschid treated you—
and you Faisal's intended wife!'

Now was her opportunity to tell Zahra the truth, but
before she could do so, Zahra continued impulsively, 'I
shall tell Raschid how wrong he was, Felicia. I cannot
allow you to take the blame for my folly, and Raschid
shall apologise to you for what he said.'

Her lips trembled and Felicia felt moved to pity, guessing how much it had hurt the younger girl to see her
adored uncle revealed in his true colours. In that moment
she felt immeasurably older than the Felicia who had
arrived in Kuwait such a short time ago. She comforted
Zahra as best she could, promising that the now despised
garments would be suitably disposed of and reminding
her that she herself had added insult to injury by deliberately goading Raschid, but Zahra was not convinced. She
shook her head sorrowfully.

'He wanted to shame you before us, Felicia. I could see
it in his eyes, but instead he shamed me!' Her voice thick-
ened on fresh tears. 'I thank Allah that I witnessed his
contempt, for I could not bear it if Saud had looked upon
me in the way Raschid did you.'

It saddened Felicia to hear the pain in her voice, but she could offer scant comfort, aside from pointing out that Raschid had his reasons for not liking her.

'Because he does not want Faisal to marry you? Felicia, promise me you will not let Raschid drive you from us. You have become very precious to me and already I think of you as a sister. Raschid will come round, I know it!'

The next day brought the noisy arrival of Nadia and her husband with their small son. Several years older than Felicia, she was a smaller, feminine version of Faisal, complete with his white smile and soft brown eyes, and yet the familiarity between brother and sister sparked off no emotion in her, Felicia discovered.

Her little boy, however, captured her heart, and before he had been in the house five minutes, Felicia was completely under his spell, listening delightedly to his important chatter as he followed her to her room. He exhibited none of the shyness of his European contemporaries, his large brown eyes frankly curious as he wandered around her room. He found the tissue-wrapped parcel she had stuffed in a corner of her empty suitcase and forgotten, and insisted on seeing what was inside and was, in fact, engaged on carefully removing the contents when Nadia walked in.

She raised her eyebrows and smiled, dropping carelessly on to the divan in the same cross-legged pose as Umm Faisal. Far more Western in outlook than either her mother or her sister, she had, nevertheless, the aura of a sheltered Eastern woman. She ruffled little Zayad's dark hair affectionately as he staggered towards her, relieving him of the package.

'A present?'

'Something someone gave me in error,' Felicia heard herself saying stiffly, changing the subject quickly. 'You must be excited about Zahra's marriage.'

'Not as much as I was about my own.' Nadia chuckled reminiscently. 'It seems strange to remember that there was ever a time when I didn't want to marry Achmed.' She saw Felicia's look of surprise and nodded her head. 'Oh yes, I was a rebel when I was younger. Our marriage was arranged before my father's death, and I plagued Raschid to free me from it. I even threatened to starve myself if he refused.'

'What happened?' Felicia enquired, intrigued. She could not imagine any female getting the better of Raschid, but plainly Nadia was perfectly happy in her marriage, and she was curious to know how this had come about.

Nadia smiled ruefully.

'It was all Raschid's doing, bless him! You will have heard of the *siyasa* on which we pride ourselves? Well, when I refused point blank to marry Achmed—and you must bear in mind that this was at the start of the month of Ramadan with the wedding only weeks away, for it was to be celebrated at the same time as the feast of Eid al-Fitr which marks the end of our fast—Raschid did not attempt to argue or reason with me. Instead he told me that he had arranged for Achmed to visit the house and that if I positioned myself in his bedroom and looked out on to the courtyard I would see Achmed arrive. He begged me to wait until then before demanding to be freed of our betrothal.' She spread her hands, laughingly. 'What could I do? I agreed.'

'And?' pressed Felicia breathlessly.

Nadia laughed again.

'And when I saw this outstandingly handsome young man walk nervously into the courtyard I knew my protests had been those of a maid who fears the intimacies of marriage, but when I looked into Achmed's face and saw gentleness and understanding there I knew there was nothing to fear. Raschid knew me better than I knew myself.' Her eyes softened into an expression of shining pleasure. 'I will say only this to you, Felicia. There are those of your race, and mine too, who anticipate their marriage vows, tossing away the kernel of the grain and keeping only the worthless husk, but there is no freedom, no equality that equals the pleasure of sharing the mysteries of one's body with the husband of one's heart, and knowing that those mysteries are revealed for him and him alone.'

The soft words almost moved Felicia to tears, expressing as they did sentiments she had always cherished but never been able to utter. In complete understanding they looked at one another, and Felicia knew that whatever Raschid might choose to believe of her, Nadia had guessed the truth.

As she got up to go, she pressed Felicia's hand lightly. 'Zahra tells me that Raschid has greatly wronged you. For her own sake she must tell him the truth, but he is a proud man, and apologising will not come easy. You will bear this in mind?'

And make it easy for him? Was that what Nadia was asking? Raschid was lucky in his family, Felicia thought enviously; they held him in high esteem.

'You are very like Raschid's grandmother,' Nadia sighed. 'But Zahra will already have told you this. My mother tells me that you and Faisal are friends.'

Sensing what was coming, Felicia said hurriedly, 'Can we talk of this at a later date—after Zahra's birthday? Nothing must be allowed to overshadow that.'

'Indeed not,' Nadia allowed, smiling, as she led her son away for his afternoon rest.

Felicia soon discovered that all the family shared Zahra's love of the oasis, and the luxurious home Raschid's grandfather had built there for his English wife. In the desert the family reverted to the ways of their ancestors, with the women gathering every morning to chat and drink coffee while Raschid and Achmed inspected the fruit farm on the other side of the oasis, and exercised the fiery Arab horses stabled in one of the outer courtyards. Zayad had attached himself to Felicia, following her wherever she went, much to the amusement of Nadia.

The day before Zahra's birthday, when the men were

out riding a messenger arrived from Saud's family inviting
the ladies to drive over. Felicia was rather dubious as to
whether or not the invitation was meant to include her,
but Zahra and Nadia overruled her protests.

When the men returned, Zahra rushed to tell them the
news. She exhibited no shyness in the presence of her
brother-in-law, who in turn treated her with brotherly
indulgence. Felicia liked Nadia's husband. He was all the
things she had once thought Faisal—kind, gentle, tender
to his wife and affectionate with his son. Against her will
her eyes were drawn to Raschid's remote figure. How
would he treat a wife? Never with tenderness!

He said something to Zahra and the younger girl
shrugged and moved away. There was an air of constraint
between them, and Felicia was sorry that Zahra had been
disillusioned. From Nadia she knew that Zahra intended
to confront Raschid with the truth, but she suspected that
she was hoping for a more propitious moment. These
seldom came, as Felicia knew from experience. She was
still hoping to find a tactful way of breaking the news that
she must soon return home. It was bound to cause speculation. Her original visit had had no time limit and it was
generally accepted by Umm Faisal that she would stay
with them until Faisal returned. That was no longer possible. Tonight she must write to him.

'And is Felicia looking forward to meeting Saud's
family?' Achmed asked with a twinkle. 'You know, of
course, how highly placed in Government circles they are?'

'Saud cares nothing for his family's prominence,' Zahra
explained selfconsciously, but Felicia could tell that the
younger girl was deliberately playing down Saud's importance.

'Now you see why it is so important that our family
observes the proprieties,' Raschid drawled. 'Already in
certain religious quarters there is unrest because our
government has brought in so many modern reforms, such
as education for women, to name but one. The greatest
tact is needed in equating the needs of the flesh with those

of the spirit, and if a member of a prominent family were seen to be flouting the unwritten rules of behaviour it could be interpreted in some quarters as a direct contravention of the Koran itself. Zahra is especially vulnerable through her connection with me. Have you forgotten that I am Christian?' he demanded.

Felicia had. She also saw much more than she had seen before.

'There is a letter for you, Miss Gordon,' Raschid added. 'From Faisal. If you will come to my study . . .'

'Raschid, if you have a moment there is something I should like to discuss with you,' Zahra interrupted hurriedly. 'I will come with you, Felicia, and then when Raschid has given you your letter he and I can talk.'

In vain Felicia tried to catch her eye to tell her that there was no need for her to confess her guilt to Raschid. As far as she was concerned the matter was over and done with, and besides, she doubted that anything would be gained by telling him the truth. Far better that Zahra put the episode completely behind her, but Zahra avoided her warning look and got to her feet, scattering silk-covered cushions.

'Overspent your allowance again?' Raschid commented humorously, opening the door for them.

'Will you see Saud tomorrow, when we visit his family?' Felicia asked Zahra as they walked behind Raschid.

She shook her head.

'That would not be permitted. In fact we should not see one another at all until he lifts the veil from my face during the wedding ceremony, but you will find our visit interesting. His family own an old fortress about two hours' drive from the oasis, and his father still likes to spend at least a part of the year in the desert.' She hesitated as Raschid disappeared into his study.

'There's still time to change your mind, you know,' Felicia pointed out gently, but Zahra shook her head.

'No, I've made up my mind. Let's go in.'

In silence Felicia took her letter from Raschid's outstretched hand, her eyes telling Zahra that there was still time for her to back down if she wished, but the younger girl resolutely ignored her, placing herself in front of Raschid, hands clasped together, head bent.

As she closed the door gently behind her, Felicia heard him say indulgently,

'So, and what is this urgent matter you wish to discuss with me, little one?'

Little one! Just for a moment Felicia felt like a child herself—the child she had once been, deprived of love and affection, forced to see others more fortunate blessed with what was denied her. And then she shook the feeling off and retired to her room to read Faisal's letter.

The words seemed to leap angrily off the paper, a bitter jumble of accusations and demands, and even when she had read it twice Felicia could barely take it in. She supposed she had Raschid to thank for this, she thought bitterly, as she read it yet again, some of the more condemnatory phrases sticking in her mind.

'Your wanton behaviour . . . encouraging my uncle to behave in the most familiar fashion . . . making a laughing stock of my reputation. . . .' These were but a few of Faisal's accusations, revealing how very thin his veneer of Westernisation actually had been. The letter finished quite abruptly, and Felicia read the last paragraph slowly.

'. . . and in view of your totally disgraceful behaviour I am forced to say that I can no longer countenance any marriage between us. I am writing to my uncle separately to inform him of my decision, and I am sure once it is known to him he will lose no time in sending you back to England, where you may parade yourself on the streets for the whole world to see without causing me to lose face.'

He had never really loved her, Felicia thought with a sigh, crumpling the letter into a small ball and throwing it into her wastepaper bin. She could not blame him entirely. She was as much at fault as he—and yet it hurt to read his letter, to know that Raschid had quite deliberately written to him showing her in a bad light—it must have been Raschid, it could be no one else. How would she have felt if she had in truth loved Faisal? What would her feelings have been at this moment? And yet she could not deny that it would be a relief not to have to pretend any longer. No doubt as soon as Raschid heard from Faisal he would lose no time in sending her home. Bitter pain shafted through her. She did not want to leave this country. Strangely enough, what hurt far more than Faisal's desertion was the knowledge that Raschid had deliberately gone behind her back and betrayed her. And yet why should he be so surprised? Hadn't he promised that he would find a way of parting them? If only he had waited a little longer he need not have put himself to the trouble. Time had achieved his ends for him, without any help. The love she thought so strong in the gentle climate of England had soon shrivelled in the merciless heat of the desert.

She took a deep breath and then another. Outside her bedroom window the swimming pool shimmered temptingly, blue as a turquoise stone set into the paved courtyard. Raschid had had it installed, so Zahra had told her, and its coolness drew her, as though somehow its silken caress could wash away her pain and hurt. Like a wounded animal she sought oblivion—not from Faisal's betrayal, which had taken second place in her chaotic thoughts, but from the new, dangerously hurtful knowledge that when she left Kuwait, she would leave behind a part of herself—in the hard uncaring hands of his uncle!

How it had happened she did not know. Nor why her senses should be enslaved to the one man who had no use or desire for her, but now the truth was inescapable. She refused to use the word 'love' in conjunction with her feelings for Raschid, but neither could she continue to deny its existence. All her heart-searching, all her reluctance to leave Kuwait had their roots in the same hidden depths of her being which had given birth to the sensual

excitement she had experienced at Raschid's touch. She
was attracted to him, she told herself; nothing more. But
it *was* more than attraction. That could not account for
the driving need within her. The ache to touch and be
touched; the burning, hurting desire that kept her awake
at night.

She glanced in the mirror, barely recognising the white
face staring back at her. She found her black swimsuit,
deeming it more suitable than her bikini, unaware of how
it accentuated her curves, flattering her slim shape, drawing attention to the valley between her breasts, the silky
sheen of her skin. As she pulled it on she realised that in
the move from Kuwait she had forgotten to buy herself a
fresh supply of salt tablets. She shrugged. It hardly
mattered now. She would not be here much longer—just
as long as it took Raschid to read Faisal's letter. She did
not think he would allow her to stay under his roof one
moment more than necessary, birthday celebrations or
no!

Although he might not know it, Raschid had won. How
ironic that it should be Faisal who was responsible for his
victory; the same Faisal who had sent her out here in the
first place to win his uncle over. It seemed that Raschid
had known Faisal far better than she had done.

It was hot outside, away from the protective shelter of
the house. The pool shimmered under the bright sun.
Felicia dived in, the water like cool silk against her heated
skin. She swam a couple of lengths, then turned over to
float luxuriously on her back, her hair a bright cloud of
molten fire against the vivid blue of the water. She closed
her eyes, letting her tense muscles relax. In the distance
she could hear voices raised in angry protest, but they
faded and then there was only the benevolent heat of the
sun and the soothing slap of the water against the sides of
the pool.

As she lay there she wondered idly why neither Nadia
nor Zahra used the pool, and then dismissed the thought,
as she struck out for the far side in a lazy crawl.

She trod water for a few seconds, trying to find the energy to haul herself out. Her eyes stung from the chlorine in the water and she closed them, rubbing them with one hand.

Someone grasped her arms, hauling her unceremoniously out of the water, to stand at the side of the pool dripping moisture on to soft leather boots.

Her eyes travelled upwards. Wide trousers were tucked into the boots, a dark cloak flung back from broad shoulders.

'Miss Gordon!'

'Raschid!' Awareness shivered through her. Was this it? Was he going to tell her that she was going home?

She forced herself to look up into his face. His expression was forbidding, his mouth tight, although whether with distaste or anger she could not tell.

'I was on my way to the stables when I saw you here.'

Felicia gritted her teeth, willing him to get to the point. Tears were not very far away, but she comforted herself with the knowledge that after today she would probably never need to endure his anger again. Oddly, it brought her no relief.

'What were you doing in the pool?'

She stared at him. 'Do I have to have your permission before I can swim now?'

His glance impaled her, sending sharp splinters of apprehension through her trembling body. Her wrap was on the other side of the pool, and she glanced helplessly at it, wishing for its admittedly frail protection against the steely thrust of his eyes.

Even the doves seemed to have ceased their endless cooing and in the unnerving silence she felt sure he must hear the frightened thudding of her heart. His eyes searched her face, looking for she knew not what, and then, as though satisfied, he smiled coolly.

'I have been looking for you. I wish to speak to you.'

Of course he did. He wanted to gloat over Faisal's defection, no doubt.

Head held high, she refused to let him see how she felt. 'I'll go and get changed, and. . . .'

He forestalled her, his touch on her deceptively light. 'I think not. What I wish to say to you requires privacy, and where better than here in the seclusion of this court-yard, where none will disturb us, since it is my own private domain.'

CHAPTER EIGHT

'Yours?'

The word trembled between them, as Raschid inclined his head in sardonic acknowledgement.

'In my country, Miss Gordon, a woman does not flaunt herself unclad before male eyes—but I have already told you this. This pool and courtyard are part of my own private quarters—but then I'm sure you know that already.'

What on earth was he accusing her of now? Despite his suave manner Felicia had the distinct impression that he was battling with overpowering rage, and yet she could not understand why this should be so.

'I'm sorry if I intruded into your private domain,' she apologised stiffly, but he swept the words aside, his mouth twisting contemptuously.

'Oh, come, you can do better than that. It seems that I owe you an apology for the other night, and opportunist that you are, I'm sure you are aware that I would have to seek you out to tender it. Where better than here, where we could not be disturbed; where the enticement of your unclad body can tempt my instincts to overrule my common sense? I am a man as any other, Miss Gordon, and no more immune than they to the charms you so provocatively display, in that apology for a swimsuit.'

A note of iron had entered his voice as his glance burned over her, but it was lost on the girl standing at his side, filled with a growing indignation and longing only to be free of the smooth voice and its hateful insinuation. She forgot about Faisal and his letter, and why she had assumed that Raschid had sought her out, and demanded,

'Are you suggesting that I deliberately came down here to entice you?' Incredulity sharpened her normally soft

voice, but Raschid seemed unaware of her heated cheeks
and flashing eyes. His mouth curled cynically.

'Are *you* suggesting that you did not?' He shook his
head. 'There is no need for pretence between us, Miss
Gordon.' He lowered his head suddenly, grasping a
handful of half damp hair and twisting it round his hand,
imprisoning her.

As she struggled his grip tightened inexorably, propelling her towards him until there was nothing between them
but the flimsy barrier of her swimsuit, and not even that
where it plunged seductively to reveal the taut thrust of
her breasts.

Her muffled protest was lost. She could feel the heat
coming off Raschid's skin. She arched desperately away
from him, but his strength was the greater and her
tired muscles were forced to concede victory and allow
him to draw her slender body against the hard length of his
own. Muscle for muscle he overpowered her, her body
losing its fight to reject the punishing familiarity of his. His
shirt was open, allowing him to hold her captive against
his golden skin, her senses swimming with the emotions she
was fighting to control.

Useless to protest that she had never been held so close
to any man before, or that the intimacy he was forcing
upon her with the hard arrogance of his body was a vio-
lation of her innocence, because she knew he was beyond
all reason.

As his hands slid the straps of her swimsuit from her
shoulders she cried a protest, embarrassed colour flooding
her cheeks as he stepped back to look down at her
unprotected body. Her hands went instinctively to shield
her breasts, but he grasped her wrists, looking his fill until
her skin was on fire with rage and humiliation.

'Charming, but not necessary,' he drawled, plainly
amused. 'Faisal may have been deceived by that air of
mock modesty, but you waste it on me, Miss Gordon.'

'Miss Gordon!' Felicia swallowed mounting hysteria.
Dear God, he had the audacity to treat her body as though

it were just another of his possessions, and yet he still
called her 'Miss Gordon'!

Stiff as a figure of marble in the circle of the arms
Raschid clamped round her, she tilted her own head
upwards to meet the sardonic mockery she knew would
be written in his eyes.

'You have a strange way of apologising, Sheikh
Raschid!' She was trembling with fury, but he barely
spared her flushed face a glance; his eyes rested on the
fragile bones of her shoulders, his mouth traced a downward path that spelled destruction to her self-control.

'You think so?' he murmured, 'Perhaps I consider that
whatever reparation was necessary has been made.'

'You think I wanted *this*?' Furiously she tried to push
him away, but his hands curled into her shoulders, hauling
her against him to lie defeated against the hard wall of his
chest, her heart pounding in terror as his mouth swooped,
capturing her defenceless lips and subjecting them to
merciless plundering as they closed stubbornly against
him. Relentless pressure forced them to part. Above her
his eyes glittered as harshly as the pitiless sun in the sky,
reminding her that soon she would be gone; that soon he
must receive Faisal's letter and then there would be no
more moments such as these. . . . Then she would never
know the harsh mastery of his embrace. . . .

As though someone had murmured 'Open Sesame' her
body yielded, melting against him, her fingers curling into
the warm darkness of the hair matting his chest. He
muttered something, the blood beating up under his skin,
and then she was crushed against him, moulded to his
body, her mouth parting willingly to allow him full licence
to savour its inner sweetness.

She neither knew nor cared what she was betraying; all
that mattered was this moment, this stolen sweetness,
which she would cherish for the rest of her life, the feel of
Raschid against her bitter-sweet as she acknowledged that
only passion stirred him. It stopped her in her tracks.
Appalled by her response, she tried to push him away,

her fingers trembling against bruised lips.

'Let me go!' She backed away, unshed tears shimmering in her eyes as she slid her swimsuit straps back over her shoulders. While she was unable to deny the cathartic effect of Raschid's lovemaking, he seemed completely unmoved by the incident. He leaned his long length against a stone pillar, his smile cruel as he surveyed her distressed state.

'Why the charade?' he asked coolly. 'You invited, I accepted. Not to have done so would have been churlish, as I'm sure you will agree.'

She invited! She had done no such thing. She told him so, half stammering with anger.

'No? You weren't hoping I would succumb to your charms and agree to your betrothal to Faisal? Wasn't that the whole purpose of your visit?' His lip curled. 'I am not a complete fool, Miss Gordon. If that was not the reason for your momentary acquiescence, then what was? I doubt my nephew would be very pleased to learn of the methods you adopt to gain my approval. What was in his letter, I wonder, to force you to such desperate measures? He wouldn't be growing tired of you, would he?'

'If he had I'm sure you would be the first to know about it,' Felicia parried, her mouth dry. So he had not heard from Faisal, but she had no doubts that his behaviour was deliberately designed to humiliate and denigrate her into giving in and returning home. She was only surprised that he had not tried bribing her into giving Faisal up, but perhaps treating her in this way afforded him some sort of satisfaction. Punishment for daring to aspire to marriage to a member of his family.

'One more thing,' he cautioned as she turned away. 'You will not run crying to Zahra of this. I do not want her birthday spoiled.'

Had he so little opinion of her that he thought she would do that, knowing how much Zahra thought of him?

She let a little of her scorn show in her voice.

'We have a saying, evil be to him who thinks evil. I wouldn't dream of hurting Zahra. I've grown very fond of her.'

'An emotion which plainly does not extend to include me.'

His audacity took her breath away. What did he expect when he treated her like some amoral gold-digger?

'An emotion which could never extend to include you,' she retorted. Never, never must he be allowed to think her momentary surrender sprang from anything other than a calculated intention to win him round to her cause. She could only hope that before he discovered that that cause had been lost long before she responded to his kiss, she would be gone, and she would not have to endure his amused contempt when he finally realised the truth.

During supper Zahra was rather subdued. Raschid had been particularly scathing about her harem outfit, she told Felicia, adding that she found her uncle changed of late, less inclined to show humorous indulgence, his temper sharper.

'When I asked him why Faisal could not come home for my birthday, he really snapped my head off. He and Faisal have never got on,' she admitted. 'Raschid thinks Faisal should be more conscious of his duty.'

A duty which no doubt included marriage to a girl of his own kind, Felicia thought wryly.

Despite the laughter at the breakfast table Felicia felt as though a lead weight were attached to her heart. She had barely slept, tossing and turning, almost at one point ready to go to Raschid and tell him that she wanted to leave, but always the thought of his contemptuous indifference held her back, making it impossible for her to confess that he had been right and she wrong.

Zahra had been thrilled with her perfume, and Felicia's thoughts turned automatically to the unopened bottle in her drawer. One day, when her heart was less tender, she would open it, and the scent would bring back memories of that dusty alley and the feel of Raschid's hands on her skin.

All night long she had battled with her pride, and at last in the soft pearly light of the false dawn had admitted the truth. She loved Raschid. Only he had the key to awaken her dormant emotions, to draw from her a response she had never thought herself capable of giving. To no other man had she reacted as she did to Raschid. For no other man had her body quivered with deep, aching need, which overcame all her fears of rejection, built up during her lonely childhood. Raschid had the power to make her forget every single consideration but the overpowering need to satisfy the throbbing hunger his touch awoke within her.

Now she could admit that what she had felt for Faisal was merely gratitude for his attention to her. She had accepted his kisses without being stirred by them, thinking her lack of response sprang from some coldness in her nature, but Raschid had proved once and for all that this was not true. With Faisal she had always been passive, content to follow his lead, but in Raschid's arms she knew a longing to be consumed by the fierce passion of which she knew instinctively he was capable. Those fires would never burn for her. She knew that now, and every instinct for self-preservation warned her to flee before Raschid discovered her vulnerability.

She closed her eyes, her face pale, startled when Nadia asked anxiously if she was all right.

All right! She smiled hollowly. She doubted if she would ever be 'all right' again, but since she could not say so she smiled weakly and brushed aside Nadia's kind concern.

The fortress owned by Saud's family was a huge pile of stone perched grimly on a rocky outcrop and commanding excellent views of the surrounding countryside—a reminder of the days when his forebears would have lived by preying off unwary travellers or other tribes daring or desperate enough to cross their territory.

Here the old ways still held sway. They drove in under

a formidable stone gateway and the women were led to a
side entrance, barely discernible. Following Umm Faisal's
example, Felicia removed her slippers as they entered the
dark cavernous hallway.

Saud's mother came forward to greet them. The traditional Arabic welcome and prayers for a long and healthy
life were exchanged. The visitors were led to opulent
cushions spread about the room, Felicia's muscles protesting a little as she tried to imitate the grace of the others.

In addition to Saud's mother there were various aunts
and cousins, all of whom had to be introduced to the
visitor from England, although Felicia was aware that
their real interest was, quite naturally, in Zahra.

It was Nadia who whispered to her that to mention the
marriage before it was a fait accompli was to put the 'evil
eye' upon it, but there was no mistaking the value of the
expensive gifts they pressed upon a blushing Zahra.

One of the women, obviously very old, commanded
Felicia to come forward.

'That is Saud's grandmother,' Nadia whispered. 'She
has seen six sons die in defence of their country, and even
His Highness puts great store by her advice.'

Felicia could well understand why. Despite the simplicity of her clothes, the strangeness of her henna-patter-
ned hands and feet, Felicia knew she was in the presence
of great wisdom. Although she spoke very little English,
her eyes were shrewd as they assessed Felicia's slender
beauty. She said something in Arabic to Umm Faisal,
who responded:

'She said that you are very like the English girl who
married her third cousin—she means Raschid's grandfather.'

The visit seemed to last for a long time. A maid came
round a second time with fresh coffee. Felicia found the
ceremony endlessly fascinating. Zahra told her now to
shake her coffee cup to signify that she had had sufficient
to drink, and she also added the warning that it was considered impolite not to drink at least three of the small

cups of the beverage.

Arabs placed great store by hospitality and ritual, as
Felicia was coming to learn, and to refuse what was given
so graciously could be considered a grave insult.

The visit was obviously a formal one, but when the
other ladies rose to leave, Umm Faisal and Zahra were
invited to stay on. Nadia touched Felicia's arm, indicating
that she leave with her.

'Raschid is discussing the final arrangements for Zahra's
dowry; Saud's mother will want to talk about the wedding, so you and I will walk in the courtyard and let
them get on with it.'

It was pleasantly cool in the garden, and Felicia felt
her tensed nerves relax for the first time since the previous
day.

'You do not like Raschid, do you?' Nadia asked
shrewdly, out of the blue. 'I have seen the look in your
eyes whenever he is mentioned. What is wrong? Can you
not tell me?'

'He does not approve of my ... my relationship with
Faisal,' Felicia admitted, glad of the opportunity to un-
burden herself. 'He thinks me a woman of the very worst
sort—avaricious, designing. ... It is natural for him to
want to protect your brother. ...'

'But not natural to be so blind,' Nadia interposed softly.
'Not Raschid, whose astuteness is fabled within our
family. He treats you as he treats no other woman, Felicia.
You must know of his English blood? He has learned to
guard his heart well, so that it is like an inner courtyard,
its beauties revealed only to a privileged few.'

Felicia's heart ached with the weight of a thousand
unshed tears. The delights Nadia's words painted so
vividly were not for her.

'Raschid has no interest in me, other than an overriding
desire for me to return home,' Felicia told her quietly.
'And were it not for the fact that if I left now it would
spoil some of Zahra's pleasure in her birthday, I assure
you I would already be gone.'

'Zahra is fond of you,' Nadia agreed. 'But as to your presence here, that is as Allah wills it.'

No, it was as Raschid willed it, Felicia thought despairingly. He alone had the power to banish her at will! If only she dared confide in Nadia and beg her help. She still had some of her savings left. Perhaps if she could borrow her fare from Nadia she could repay in within a few months if she was really careful with her budget. She started to speak, but Nadia stopped her. 'Quickly!' she urged. 'We must return to the harem.'

She whisked Felicia inside so quickly that she barely had time to comprehend what was happening, before Nadia was pulling her veil across her face and hurrying her away.

In the distance she caught the sound of male voices, footsteps ringing across the courtyard they had so recently vacated.

'That was a close call!' Nadia breathed. 'Living away from home I tend to be less strict with myself, but it would have shamed Raschid before Saud's father had we been discovered in the garden. Achmed would have been furious with me.' She made a small moue. 'Fortunately I heard them coming in time. I'm trying to persuade Raschid to take us all out hawking. It used to be his favourite pastime, and his falcons are a sight to behold. It will be the last time we are all together as a family before Zahra marries, and it seems fitting that we should revert to the freedom of our childhood years, if only for a few hours.'

'In that case you won't want me along,' Felicia began, but Nadia swept her protests aside.

'Of course we shall want you.' She bent forward and kissed Felicia's cheek. 'You are a delight to us all, Felicia, and far too unassuming, although I hope Zahra does not speak the truth when she says that you may marry Faisal. Although he is my brother, I have to admit that he is weak, too changeable in his ways to make a good husband. Not like my Achmed.' She glanced speculatively at

Felicia. 'You know, in a way I am surprised that you do not get on well with Raschid. He has always been a great admirer of beauty, and you have much of that. Also your manner cannot help but please; you are of his religion.'

'Liking does not come from any of those things,' Felicia said shakily, trying to stem the flood of longing Nadia's words had aroused. 'It comes from the heart, and Raschid's heart is closed to me.' This was her chance to beg Nadia for her aid, but she was too shy to ask, and by the time they had returned to the others it was too late.

Later, she was to regret her weakness, but when they joined the rest of their party, her own worries subsided in the general excitement over Zahra's wedding.

It was late when they started back. Somehow or other Felicia found herself travelling with Raschid, sitting in the front seat while Umm Faisal and Zahra occupied the back.

He was concentrating on the road, a barren landscape in black and silver, and she stole a glance at his remote profile, swept by a wave of love. Where on earth Nadia had got the idea that he could feel anything but disdainful contempt for her, Felicia could not imagine. She sighed, letting weary eyelids drop over aching eyes.

The land had already cast its timeless spell over her, and the man. . . . She looked again at his shadowed profile. His head turned and their eyes met, pleasure and pain mingled as another fierce wave of longing swamped her.

At last she had given her feelings their rightful name—she loved Raschid, against all the odds, in spite of the unbridgable gulfs of background and upbringing that yawned between them, she loved him.

She sighed as tiredness drained even the ability to think properly. She might as well love the sun or the moon. Her eyes closed and opened as she struggled against waves of exhaustion. At her side Raschid turned and frowned.

'It has been a long day for you, Miss Gordon. My sister

and Zahra are both sleeping. Feel free to join them if you wish. We have a good hour's journey in front of us.'

They were following Achmed and Nadia, and as he spoke the powerful headlights of the Mercedes picked out the car in front quite clearly—and its occupants, Nadia's dark head cradled on Achmed's shoulder. An aching longing so intense that it was almost a physical pain hit her. She longed to cry out against it, stifling it, but the sound was trapped in her throat. She fought to subdue the urge to move closer to Raschid, to place her head on his shoulder and know she would not be rebuffed.

Pride alone kept her upright in her seat, her eyes sliding away from Nadia and Achmed, but it was Raschid who said curtly:

'You're practically falling asleep sitting up, Miss Gordon. If pride prevents you from using my shoulder as a pillow, try telling yourself that very soon I shall be your uncle and capable of commanding your obedience. I know you detest me, but this road is very uneven in parts. If you fall asleep as you are you could easily be thrown against a window or do yourself some other injury, so let common sense take the place of pride and accept my offer in the spirit in which it is given.'

What could she do? Even so, she had not expected his arm to curve round her, pulling her against the warmth of his body, and in response to her unvoiced question he said curtly:

'I am perfectly able to drive with one hand—this is not a busy road, and I am not a young fool intent on showing off. Try to relax, I do not intend to harm you.'

But he was doing, whether he intended it or not. Merely the pressure of his body as he changed gear, the warm male smell of his flesh, harmed her irreparably as her heart wept for the unattainability of its one desire. She drew a steady breath and instantly her nostrils were full of the masculine odour of his body. She closed her eyes, but with his hard shoulder beneath her cheek, it was impossible to banish the tormenting image of his mouth, its well cut lines as well known to her as the softer shape of her own.

She fought against sleep as long as she could, not wanting it to steal from her these precious moments when Raschid gave his strength unstintingly, but the warmth of his body made her drowsy and her tormented senses were not proof against the smothering waves of sleep. Her body relaxed, her head falling against his shoulder. His arm tightened holding her steady, as they drove into the endless night of the desert.

Felicia had no clear recollection of their arrival. Sleepy and bemused, she stumbled from the car, and Raschid's strong arm caught her as she fell.

She thanked him, returning awareness making her desperate to avoid the sharpness of his eyes.

Sleepily Umm Faisal offered a cup of coffee, but Felicia refused. Like a greedy miser, she wanted to gloat over her precious hoard of happiness to fall asleep, dreaming of those sacred moments when Raschid's arms had held her without anger or punishment.

It was quiet in the courtyard. Zahra was with Umm Faisal. With the month of Ramadan fast approaching the arrangements for the weddding had to be finalised. Only that morning Umm Faisal had shown Felicia the soft rose silk from which Zahra's bridal caftan would be fashioned. Shimmering threads of beaten silver flashed in the sunlight, and Felicia fingered the fabric in awe.

Later Zahra had shown her the gifts Saud had sent her—the silver and turquoise hand jewellery handed down through seven generations of his family, necklaces of beaten gold studded with rubies, rings and ankle bracelets, a whole treasure trove of precious and semi-precious stones guaranteed to excite the most prosaic female imagination.

Lastly Zahra produced an intricately worked girdle of beaten silver. This was the symbolic girdle used to fasten the bride's shift, she explained, and once it *was* fastened in place, none but her bridegroom had the right to remove it.

'Raschid still has the girdle made for his grandmother,' Zahra told her, 'and although he is Christian, he will marry according to the laws of our faith as well, for that was his grandfather's wish, thus the two religions will live side by side in harmony with one another.'

Every mention of Raschid brought nervous tension to Felicia's body. Every day she expected to be summoned to his study and told that he had heard from Faisal. Why did she torture herself like this? Why did she not go to him and ask to be sent home before he discovered the truth about why she had been content to linger long after she knew of Faisal's change of heart? Her own heart gave her the answer. She was sitting by the fishpond, staring lazily into space. A tortoiseshell carp jumped in the water, showering her with tiny droplets; in the distance doves cooed; even the perfect symmetry of the house echoed the same pervasive sense of peace. Her red-gold head bent over the pool, unaware that she was being observed by the man who stood in the shade of the lime trees the fragile vulnerability of her lightly tanned skin exposed to his searching gaze. His expression unfathomable, he continued to watch, and then turned abruptly, his progress across the courtyard fluttering the doves into noisy protest. Felicia glanced up, her expression unguarded, unable to quench the fierce joy running through her veins.

'Sheikh Raschid!' There was even pleasure in saying his name.

He inclined his head in the manner which had become so familiar that it was engraved on her heart. A small pang shot through her, and a hesitant smile quivered on her lips, as she suppressed her alarm.

'Have you heard from Faisal?'

Now what had made her ask that? His brows drew together in blank disapproval.

'No,' he replied curtly. 'Are you missing him so much that you are willing to beg *me* for news of him? Perhaps I did you an injustice. Perhaps you do care for him after all.'

Now was her chance to tell him the truth. The words trembled on her lips, only to be silenced as he added cynically, 'However, as we both know, appearances can be deceptive. Our strong sun darkens the colour of your skin to the colour of ours, but it cannot change what lies underneath. There can be no happiness in a marriage between yourself and Faisal.'

'East and West can live in harmony,' Felicia protested. 'Your own grandparents. . . .'

'They were an exception,' Raschid interrupted curtly. 'My grandmother willingly gave up everything to be with my grandfather. Can you honestly tell me that your love for Faisal possesses that strength? Would you willingly wander the desert with him, an outcast to your own people?'

Her eyes gave him the answer. Not for Faisal, but for him. . . . She would willingly walk barefoot to hell and back for him. She longed to reach out and touch him, to slide her fingers through the dark crispness of his hair, to kiss those firmly chiselled lips and to urge that lean body to take her and make her a part of him, her flesh yielding and melting into his as his hard hands possessed her. She closed her eyes and prayed as she had never prayed before, that she might banish these tormenting images.

When she opened them again Raschid was watching her dispassionately. 'It is not safe for you to walk alone out here, Miss Gordon,' he warned her.

'In case I might be carried off by some desert barbarian, do you mean? Surely *they* would scorn me as you do, as being worthless and of little account. An unwanted intruder in their lives; a female of no virtue whose life means no more than a few grains of sand.'

'Faisal did not scorn you,' Raschid pointed out. 'And it is after all, he who holds your heart, is it not?'

She watched him disappear into the shadows, her body aching as though she had been beaten; which metaphorically she felt as though it had. She herself had lashed it unmercifully with the reminder that Raschid cared nothing for her.

All her pleasure in the garden was gone. She went to her room, drawn to the drawer where she had concealed the small phial of perfume. Almost against her will she unstoppered it, and the fragrant, fresh smell of the English countryside stole through the room, coupled with a scent almost bitter-sweet, but faintly haunting, so in tune with her emotions that she could only marvel at the perfume blender's ability to correctly judge her mood and transform it into this perfume which would always bring home to her the senselessness of unwanted love.

CHAPTER NINE

PROMPTED by Achmed, Raschid had made arrangements to entertain his guest by taking him hawking, a trip which could take two or three days dependent on the game to be had.

Nadia had begged Achmed to intercede with Raschid on behalf of the female half of the household, declaring that it was unfair that they should be left behind while the men enjoyed themselves.

The plan was that the men would take Raschid's falcons, a couple of servants and two Land Rovers to hold all their gear and spend a couple of days relaxing in the desert.

Nadia explained to Felicia that in their younger days she and Zahra had often accompanied Raschid on these trips, revelling in the freedom from routine these outings provided.

'In the old days the men used tents, like the Badu, cooking over an open fire, but nowadays things are a bit more civilised. We use sleeping bags and camping Gaz,' Nadia laughed. 'Raschid does not really approve. He still prefers to follow the old ways of our people, but Mother used to worry that Faisal would burn himself or get indigestion from half cooked food and so, in the end, Raschid had to give in.'

Even so it sounded enviably exciting—the wide open spaces of the desert, men in long white robes, eating under a dark blue velvet sky studded with stars. Felicia gave a faint sigh. Uncle George had never approved of picnics, or indeed eating out of doors at all.

'Don't worry, Achmed will be able to persuade Raschid. He'll have to,' she added with a darkling look, 'otherwise I've told him he won't be going himself.'

Felicia burst out laughing. Nadia was so refreshingly

modern in her outlook, and it was plain that Achmed
adored her.

He came into the women's quarters while they were
watching Zayad's antics, a beaming smile splitting his
face.

'Raschid has agreed that you girls can come with us.
Not without an awful lot of persuasion, I might add, and
I'd better warn you, we mean to set off after first light
tomorrow, and Raschid is in no mood to make allowances
for you. He says if you are to come with us you must
expect to be treated just like the men.'

'Isn't that just typical of him?' Nadia complained. 'I
swear he thinks more of his falcons than he does of us.'

'Quite probably,' Achmed agreed cheerfully. He looked
thoughtfully at Felicia, who was trying to play cat's
cradles with Zayed. 'This will be your first trip into the
interior of the desert, won't it? Nadia will tell you what to
take along.' He frowned and seemed to hesitate.

Had Raschid expressed doubts about the wisdom of
taking her along because *she* was to be a member of the
party? A casual enquiry of Zahra had elicited the information that unless they sent someone to Kuwait to collect it they would receive no mail while they were in the
desert, and so, thinking herself safe for at least a few days,
Felicia had closed her mind to the heartache she was
storing up for herself, determined to make of the precious
time left to her enough memories to warm her through
the long cold years ahead.

A little later in the day Nadia went with her to her
room to sort out what she ought to take on the trip. 'Your
jeans, I think,' she announced, pursing her lips, 'and a
long-sleeved blouse. I think I have riding boots that will
fit you. When the falcons are hunting the hubara we shall
have to follow on foot, and boots protect the ankles and
legs from snakes and scorpions.'

'Raschid didn't want us to go because of me, didn't he?'
Felicia interrupted quietly, needing to know the answer,
in spite of the pain it might cause.

Nadia looked uncomfortable, and Felicia knew she had guessed correctly. 'It is just that it is our custom for each girl to be accompanied by a man to watch over her safety,' Nadia explained, 'and in Faisal's absence Raschid is very conscious of his responsibility towards you. Zahra and I are accustomed to the desert. You are not.' Her smile softened the words. 'Don't worry, Felicia, we shall take care of you, but try to understand. . . .'

'To understand what? That your uncle considers me an unwanted nuisance? I understand *that* already.'

Nadia bit her lip, her eyes clouded. 'Forgive me, Felicia, but this hostility you feel towards Raschid—could it be that you use it to mask other—very different emotions?'

One look at Nadia's face told her that the older girl had guessed the truth. Pride made her grasp at any straw, however frail, to conceal her feelings.

'If you mean love, I consider that any woman who fell in love with your uncle would need to be either a fool or a masochist!'

Felicia saw with relief that Nadia was staring at her in stunned surprise, but it was several seconds before she realised why. When Nadia continued to stare over her shoulder, the hairs at the back of her neck began to prickle warningly, and she swung round just in time to see Raschid's coldly furious expression as he strode past the door.

'Do you think he heard me?'

Nadia recovered her voice, nodding her head comiseratingly. 'I'm so sorry. I never heard him until it was too late.'

Felicia shrugged, trying to tell herself that it did not matter; another stone on the wall separating herself and Raschid was hardly likely to make much difference one way or the other.

'It doesn't matter,' she assured Nadia. 'After all, he's never made any pretence of liking me. In fact I'm sure he's feeling exceptionally pleased with the results of his eavesdropping. He'll be more positive than ever now that I'm everything he thought, and worse!'

'Let me explain to him,' Nadia suggested, but Felicia shook her head decisively. What was there to explain? That Nadia had accused her of being in love with him, and in order to defend herself she had claimed that no woman could be? He would know she was lying.

'What's the point? Let him think what he likes.'

'It's all my fault,' Nadia admitted apologetically. 'I shouldn't have teased you in the first place. I am sorry.'

When Nadia had gone Felicia stared at her clothes hanging in the wardrobe. Soon it would be empty. They would not be staying at the oasis much longer, and once Faisal's letter reached Raschid, she would have to face the day of reckoning. If only she did not have to apply to Faisal's family in order to get home! She was not left with even that shred of pride intact.

As Achmed had foretold, Raschid lost no time in announcing that if the girls were intent on accompanying them, they would have to present themselves in the outer courtyard at first light.

That had been last night, and now, pulling on her jeans in the pearly light of the false dawn, Felicia rubbed the sleep from her eyes. Below, in the courtyard, she could hear sounds of activity. Tiredly she brushed her hair, securing it with a ribbon. Following Nadia's advice she added a thick, chunky sweater to the absolute necessities Raschid had limited them to—a change of underwear, a clean blouse, some soft woollen socks to wear inside Nadia's boots, and a pair of sunglasses.

She could see a couple of menservants loading things into the two Land Rovers parked below. Nadia had invited her to travel with herself and Achmed, and Felicia had accepted. It would be less wearing on her fragile nervous system than riding with Raschid.

Breakfast had been set out for them in one of the salons, although Felicia's stomach rebelled at the thought of yoghurt and dates before the sun had crept over the horizon.

Zayad gave them all a sticky kiss as they prepared to leave, then went docilely to his nurse.

'He's so good, isn't he?' Felicia marvelled.

'Arab children are accustomed to surrogate mothers, Miss Gordon,' Raschid said crisply from behind her. 'They have to be when daughters-in-law make their homes with their husbands' families. Unlike you in the West, we care enough about our children to give them a settled background so that they can grow up secure in the love of their family.'

It was an unjust accusation, and hot words of rebuttal trembled on her lips, to be swallowed when she reflected that any ill-feeling between Raschid and herself was bound to spoil the enjoyment of the others. Heroically she merely gave him a polite little smile, and pushed back her chair intending to follow Nadia.

The first rays of the sun crept over the horizon, glinting on the large oval brass dish on a small table, and Felicia, her attention momentarily diverted, felt the blood freeze in her veins. In the dish lay half a dozen envelopes; the top one an airmail letter, very obviously addressed in Faisal's hand and bearing Raschid's name.

Her hand crept to her throat, she longed to reach out and pluck the letter away before it could ruin her last precious memories, but Nadia was urging her through the door and she had perforce to follow.

The morning air rang with the bustle of their departure, the strident cries of the falcons drawing Felicia's attention.

Until Nadia had mentioned it she had not realised that Raschid trained the falcons himself when he could spare the time. Even hooded, their cruel beaks and curving talons made her shudder, striking a chill right through her; the birds' scarlet jesses were blood-coloured in the early morning sun.

The bird nearest to her let out a shrill cry and flapped

its wings. The servant holding it grinned.

'Very good falcon, this one. He is named Sahud.'

Felicia raised her hand to touch the bird's tawny feathers, and instantly her fingers were seized in a crushing grip. 'Don't touch him!'

Both Zahra and Nadia looked round to see whom Raschid was addressing with such controlled fury, and Felicia's face burned beneath the open amusement of the *saggar* holding the falcon.

'Those birds cost upwards of two thousand pounds apiece, Miss Gordon,' Raschid said crushingly. 'They are trained to attack and maim anything that moves—and that includes those pretty fingers you were fluttering about in front of him.'

There was a large lump in her throat. She wanted to make a furious retort, to tell him that she thought the *saggar* had been inviting her to stroke the bird, but pride prevented her.

'No harm has been done, Raschid,' Nadia said soothingly, coming to Felicia's rescue. 'Honestly, you treat those birds like children!'

'Because like children they have to be trained to obey, and rewarded when they do so.'

A servant was handing him a leather glove, heavily embroidered with silver and gold threads, the leather as soft and supple as silk. Raschid pulled it on, smoothing it over his hand before transferring the bird from the *saggar*'s wrist to his own.

Felicia watched as he proffered it a piece of raw meat. It took it, ripping the flesh with its talons and beak. Slightly nauseated, she turned away.

Nodding to the *saggar*, Raschid handed the bird back to him.

'This is life, Miss Gordon,' he told her drily, proving that he had observed her reaction. 'In the desert one has to fight to survive.'

'And kill?' she whispered, trying not to look at the bright splash of blood on the cobbles.

'When necessary,' Raschid agreed coolly. 'Perhaps you would prefer to remain behind and keep my sister company?'

And miss the opportunity of those last remaining hours of *his* company? She shook her head, and their eyes clashed.

'Very well, on your own head be it. I warn you now, though, there will not be time to make allowances for your inexperience and ignorance of our ways.'

Nadia and Achmed were already in the Land Rover, Zahra chatting eagerly to her sister through the open window.

'Sorry, I didn't realise we were ready to leave,' Felicia apologised, hurrying towards them.

Raschid's voice halted her.

'You will be travelling with me, Miss Gordon,' he announced. 'Please get in the Land Rover. Zahra, will you go with Achmed and Nadia. Selim, Ali, one of you go with Achmed and the other come with me.'

Almost paralysed with dismay, Felicia glanced pleadingly at Nadia. 'Miss Gordon, you are keeping us waiting,' Raschid reminded her.

Nadia made a sympathetic grimace and gave her a little push.

'Go on, he won't eat you!'

There was nothing else for it. With dragging footsteps she walked across to the second Land Rover, her face resolutely averted from Raschid's masked features.

The door slammed behind her. Selim climbed into the back, reaching over to hand Raschid the pile of letters Felicia had seen in the hallway.

'Ali brought the mail when we went for the Land Rovers.'

Taking it from him, Raschid stuffed the letters on to the shelf in front of him, giving them only the most cursory glance. Faisal's letter was at the bottom, and holding her breath Felicia waited to see if he had noticed it. Apparently he had not. She opened her mouth to say that she had changed her mind and would not be going with them, but it was too late. The gates were open and as the sun finally burst over the horizon in a dazzle of molten gold they drove out into the unknown.

With every second she expected Raschid to reach for his mail, but he was concentrating on his driving, and gradually she allowed her clenched muscles to relax. They would have to stop sooner or later, and when they did. . . . She closed her eyes in despair. When they did he would read Faisal's letter and then. . . . She dragged her thoughts away, trying to concentrate on her surroundings. Even this early in the day she could feel the heat rising from the desert, and before too long her blouse was clinging stickily to her back. Only the odd remark in Arabic punctuated the silence as Selim pointed out various landmarks to Raschid.

Secretly Felicia considered that one sandhill looked very much like another, but obviously this could not be so, for several times during the course of the morning Raschid changed direction.

After a while she noticed that he always kept the sun on the left-hand side of the Land Rover, and feeling rather pleased with herself she deduced that he was using it to navigate. There was no compass in the Land Rover, but to a man used to the desert and its ways, the sun would be all the guide he needed.

This supposition was reinforced when Raschid brought the Land Rover to a halt shortly before noon, his abrupt nod confirming that she should get out. Her eyes flew instinctively to the letters, her mouth dry with apprehension.

Her clothes and face were gritty from the sand thrown up by the tires, but it was tension that was responsible for the cramped state of her limbs. She almost fell out of the jeep, and it was Raschid who saw what was happening and thrust open his door, striding round to swing her unceremoniously to the ground. Beneath lowered lashes she watched him. Hard and impassive, his face had a quality of strength that would give one confidence in him.

If one had to be lost in this vast wilderness, he would make a good companion, she thought irrelevantly. A woman could rely on his strength even when she could not hope for his tenderness.

He started to walk back to the Land Rover.

'Stiff?' Zahra teased.

'A little,' Felicia acknowledged, her eyes on Raschid. He was taking the letters from the shelf. 'Do we hunt now?' she asked Zahra absently. Was he going to open them now? Already she could hear his sardonic jeers.

'After we have eaten and had a drink. The men will put up the falcons and we will follow them in the Land Rover. Sometimes they fly several miles without spotting a single hubara. They are wily birds, because although they cannot fly great distances, they have learned how to remain immobile while the falcon flies over them, and they can also discharge a thick, slimy substance into the falcon's eyes and feathers which renders it defenceless, so you see the hunt is not all one-sided.'

Achmed's eyes twinkled.

'I can see that such a state of affairs appeals more to your British sense of fair play, Miss Gordon. Like your fox, our hubara, although a much humbler species, nevertheless has its own native cunning, which allows it to outwit its much more intelligent foe.'

Raschid hadn't spoken during this interchange, but at this he raised his head, regarding Felicia with a sardonic smile.

'I doubt if Miss Gordon would be quite as impressed with the hubara's cunning if she had to rely on its meat to survive.'

'I am not the fool you would have everyone believe me, Sheikh Raschid,' Felicia said quietly, with dignity, 'but I thought the purpose of this outing was to enjoy ourselves, not catch our dinner.'

'Touché, Miss Gordon. I doubt if Raschid has ever eaten hubara meat in his life, have you, my friend?' Achmed asked gaily.

'Then you would be wrong,' Raschid replied, without elaborating.

If only those letters had remained in Kuwait! How long would it be before he opened them? After lunch?

The falcons started to screech, sensing freedom, and the subject of hubara meat and its desirability was dropped. Accepting a cup of fresh lime juice from Zahra, Felicia sat down next to her, letting her aching limbs relax. She lay back and closed her eyes, letting her body absorb the sensations of her surroundings—the coarseness of the sand under her fingers, the heat of the sun, the faint smell of petrol, the soft murmur of Arab voices.

'What do you think of the desert, Miss Gordon?'

Raschid's voice startled her and her eyes flew anxiously to his.

There was no sign of Faisal's letter. She started to tremble, wondering if he had devised some subtle form of torture, whereby he was going to say nothing until she herself raised the subject. Very well, two could play at that game!

'It's magnificent,' she said coolly, glancing round. 'Whenever I'm here I wonder how I can endure to shut myself in an office, like an animal in a cage, but even the freest among us is chained by something; the greater our responsibilities, the greater the chains that bind us. A woman who shares the life of a man such as I has to learn to share his love for places such as these.'

'Like your grandmother, you mean?'

'She was an exception,' Raschid said curtly. 'There can be few women who would give up so much merely for the love of a man. In those days my family had no wealth as we know it today, and life was hard. I cannot see you, with your pale skin and pampered existence, forsaking life's luxuries to cleave to one man, and one alone.'

'Because you don't want to see it,' Felicia said quietly. 'You see in me only what you want to see.'

'I would to God that were possible,' Raschid said harshly, his eyes suddenly intent. 'Now you are angry,' he told her softly, 'and your eyes glint green fire as though they would consume me in their depths.' His own glittered like jet between the fringe of his lashes. 'And yet when I kissed you the other day, they were pools of mysterious jade.'

'Raschid, Felicia, are you ready to eat?'

Felicia didn't know whether to bless Nadia or to curse her. 'Ready!' she called, jumping to her feet.

They had a snack lunch prepared by the servants at the villa, and as soon as it was over the men moved over to the falcons.

'This is where we become unwanted appendages,' Nadia warned her. 'Once the birds are put up, the Land Rovers will follow. If you take my advice you will get in the front and be prepared to hold on tight. It can be a pretty hair-raising experience. It is a matter of pride not to lose a falcon, and the men don't make any allowances for female passengers.'

Felicia was glad that Zahra had warned her.

As she climbed into the Land Rover her eyes went automatically to where Raschid had placed the letters. They were gone. Her heart started to thump heavily. He must have read Faisal's letter. It could only be a matter of time before he confronted her, unless of course he *was* deliberately prolonging her agony, playing a game of cat and mouse, enjoying her mental torture. If only she had had the courage to tell him before. If only she had not let her foolish heart sway her judgment. She felt the jeep rock as Raschid climbed in. He slammed the door and switched on the engine, and then she was hanging on for grim death as the vehicle bounced and swayed over the sandhills, lurching from left to right as they followed the falcon, soaring above them, a tiny speck in the deep blue sky.

Sand clung to her eyelashes and hair. Every time she inhaled she tasted it in her mouth, the fine particles getting everywhere as the wheels threw up cloud after cloud behind them.

They crossed deep gullies and sharp inclines, at frightening speeds, the engine racing as it battled to obey Raschid's commands. At times they doubled back on themselves, and Felicia felt bruised all over as she was flung against the door and dashboard.

Selim shouted something in excitement and Felicia felt the Land Rover buck like a temperamental horse. The tiny speck disappeared. Raschid cursed, his hands tensing on the wheel as he swung the Land Rover hard over. Felicia held her breath, her fingers clinging to the dashboard. The whole world seemed to turn upside down, sand and sky rushing past the window. She was flung against the door with a jolt that drove the breath from her body, and then they were speeding across a flat plateau, sand spraying across the windscreen.

'You all right?' Raschid asked tersely.

She could only nod her head. Painful, nerve-tensing— the chase was nevertheless exhilarating, and she wouldn't have missed it for the world, she realised to her surprise.

Even when the falcon hovered motionless against the cobalt sky, dropping to earth with the swiftness of a desert night, she could feel no revulsion, only relief that the end was mercifully quick, the unfortunate hubara despatched with one efficient twist of the falcon's talons.

The *saggar* whistled tunelessly and within seconds the Land Rovers were halting, the *saggars* climbing out to wait for the falcons' return.

Exhausted but thrilled, Felicia waited while the whole business began again. She had told that the falcons could kill up to eight or nine times in one day, but as Nadia explained, Raschid thought it unfair to take so much game when they were merely hunting for pleasure, so he normally restricted his bag to two or three hubara per falcon.

She had been relieved to discover that they would not be expected to eat the results of their expedition. Although the hubara were not particularly lovable creatures, her tender heart would have found it difficult to contemplate eating their flesh, no matter how delicious it might be.

The dying sun was casting long shadows across the sand when Raschid finally called a halt. Weary but exalted, Felicia tried to relax as the Land Rover plunged through the brief Eastern dusk to a small oasis where they were going to make camp.

Raschid had suggested that they would make the return journey that night, but Nadia had demurred, and from the looks she was casting Achmed, Felicia suspected that the velvet darkness of the desert night held special memories for them that both were eager to renew.

Nadia confirmed this later when they made camp at the oasis, informing Felicia that they had spent their honeymoon in the desert, just the two of them with a tent and a Land Rover, full of equipment. 'And very romantic it was too,' Nadia confided reminiscently, rummaging for the sleeping bags. 'I'd better give these to Selim. Make the most of this trip,' she advised Felicia. 'It's the only time you will see the men making themselves useful.'

It was true. Even Raschid was pitching in helping Ali to unload boxes of food and the camping stove. It was all vaguely reminiscent of her Girl Guide days, Felicia thought, only on a far more sophisticated level.

Someone had got a fire going, feeding it with material brought from the villa, and in its flickering flames Felicia saw Raschid's face, his expression for once unguarded as he smiled down at Zahra. Her heart caught in her throat, and unbearable pain swept her because he had never looked at her like that.

As though suddenly aware of her intense scrutiny he lifted his head, his eyes blazing into hers, and she trembled on a convulsive shudder. Maybe it was as well that her self-inflicted torture would soon be brought to an end. She was beginning to appreciate the meaning of the phrase 'living on one's nerves'.

'Will the Sitt have some rice?'

It was Selim, soft-footed as a cat as he padded up to her. Felicia shook her head. Despite the fresh air and

Faisal's letter. Out of the corner of her eye she saw Ali filling Rachid's plate. Here in the desert formality went by the board. Selim and Ali moving among them, silent and hawk-eyed filling plates and coffee cups with no regard for the normal rule of male precedence, and Felicia even saw Achmed draw Nadia within the curve of his arm, feeding her tidbits from his own plate, his eyes tender as he looked down into her laughing face.

There was a huge lump in her throat.

'They are fortunate, those two,' Zahra whispered at her side. 'Tonight they will share each other's bed under the stars, at one with the universe and each other. It makes me long for my Saud.' She smiled ruefully. 'I should not say that, I know. Poor Mother would be shocked if she heard me.

'Do you ache for the one you love, Felicia?'

Silently she nodded her head, her eyes lifting instinctively to Raschid's broad shoulders. He was sitting barely a yard away, talking to Selim, obviously deep in conversation.

'Yes,' she admitted painfully, 'I do, Zahra.'

She and Zahra were to share one of the tents, while Achmed and Nadia had the other. Raschid and the servants were sleeping out in the open and after a quick dip in the oasis, Felicia was glad to crawl into her fleecy bag.

She had heard about the intense cold of the desert night, but this was the first time she had experienced it first-hand. Sleep evaded her; Raschid's face kept coming between her and the oblivion she desired. Next to her the sound of Zahra's quick, even breathing filled the tent. Outside was all the glory of the Eastern night—the stark beauty of the desert, palm trees whispering their indolent message to the night breeze; above, the dark blue velvet canopy of the sky studded with stars brighter by far than any diamonds. No wonder the wandering Badu called no man master, counting themselves more endowed with riches than any city-dwelling king.

She rolled on to her side, punching her pillow and trying to blot out the image of Raschid. Half an hour later she crawled wearily out of her sleeping bag. Her body was tired, but her mind refused to let her sleep. A short walk might help ease her tension, might help her to prepare some sort of defence against the accusations the morning was bound to bring.

Outside it was bitterly cold and she was glad of the thick sweater she had put on top of her blouse. Disregarding the boots Nadia had loaned her, she padded across the sand, breathing in the pure crystal air, and filling her lungs with its sharp freshness.

'Miss Gordon!'

She spun round. Raschid was standing by one of the Land Rovers watching her. Her heart sank. If only she had stayed in the tent! What better time than now, when they were alone, for him to confront her with her duplicity? What possible excuses could she offer for abusing their hospitality by remaining with them when she knew that Faisal no longer wanted her? Could she plead Zahra's birthday, or would he see through the protective sham and pluck the truth from her heart?

'What are you looking for, Miss Gordon? Money? Romance? Does even your mercenary little heart yearn for a man's hard arms to possess your slenderness and bind it to him, on a night like this? His lips against yours as the coldness of the desert gives way to the heat of mutual passion?'

Felicia gasped in pain, wondering if he knew how he was tormenting her. She sensed that here in the desert he was a different man from the cool, sardonic entrepreneur who ran their vast empire.

'I merely wanted to walk,' she stammered. 'I couldn't sleep. . . .'

'Because you longed so much for my nephew?' he mocked savagely. 'Well, I have longings too, and am as able to assuage your needs as Faisal—also I have the advantage of being here, while he is many miles away.' He crossed the small space dividing them and took her in his arms.

If it had wanted to punish her he must have succeeded beyond his wildest imaginings, Felicia thought despairingly, looking pleadingly up into his face for some trace of pity. In the moonlight her skin was the colour of a waxen waterlily, only her eyes glowing darkly as they searched in vain for some sign of remorse. There was none—only the hardening demand of his arms, and the cold implacable purpose in his eyes, as he bent his head, obliterating the moonlight and filling her world with darkness, his face reflecting all the cruelty of the falcon's descent to its prey.

It was impossible to resist. Impossible and unthinkable. This was her one moment stolen from time, and she admitted that in the hidden recesses of her heart she had dreamed of something like this. She longed for his touch even when it was fuelled by rage, and out here in the darkness she could pretend for a while that the arms that held her were those of a lover, that Raschid strained her body against his in desire and not anger, that the hands possessing her body trembled against her skin in passion and not fury.

She closed her eyes so that she would not see the contempt in his eyes, and gave herself up to his kiss, letting his mouth mould and teach hers. She had been kissed before—but she had never known this complete subjugation of self—this complete need to be one with another person to the extent that she was pressing herself against Raschid as though she wanted to imprint the feel of his body against her very bones.

Somehow her sweater had been removed and the buttons of her blouse unfastened, leaving her pearly skin exposed to Raschid's impatient mouth. Her own hands mutely implored closer contact with his body, her murmured protest silenced under the pressure of his mouth as it taught her the meaning of desire.

His lips trailed lazily across her cheek, nibbling the lobe of her ear, descending to caress her neck and the fragile hollows of her shoulder blade, and then lower still to the shadowy cleft between her breasts.

Her heart was beating like a trapped bird. Stupid to feel so shy and so aroused. A lassitude enveloped her; she longed for his complete possession, and arched instinctively against him. He growled deep in his throat, his hands inside the waistband of her jeans, holding her so close to him that she could feel his impatient desire, her breasts swelling tautly in answering need. Through the thin barrier of their clothes she could feel the hard maleness of him, and fire licked along her veins as she sought to convey her growing desire. A small creature moved in the undergrowth, disturbing the heavy silence of the night. Realisation shuddered through her, breaking the spell that had enchanted her. Her flesh shrank under Raschid's touch, and she felt him probing the darkness, listening . . . waiting. . . .

The moment was gone. They were no star-crossed lovers, impatient for the culmination of their urgent love-making, but two enemies using their bodies to wage a war of attrition—or at least that was what Raschid thought. What had he intended to do? Make love to her and then throw Faisal's desertion in her face? Perhaps he didn't realise that she already knew, and was deliberately leading her on, waiting until she was at her most vulnerable, to throw the truth at her.

He was not like the falcon after all, she thought; they at least killed quickly and cleanly.

'Obviously I was not a totally acceptable substitute after all,' he drawled at her side. 'A pity. You should have used your imagination a little more, or have you forgotten that I am far richer than Faisal, and far better equipped to pay for my pleasure?'

And then he was gone, melting into the darkness, leaving her to stumble back to her tent alone.

'So, did you enjoy your journey into the desert?' Umm Faisal asked Felicia.

They had arrived back just after lunch and Nadia and Achmed had gone to their own quarters with Zayad. Zahra was with the dressmaker being measured for her wedding clothes and Felicia was alone with Umm Faisal.

'Very much,' she replied listlessly. Since their return from the desert a curious inertia seemed to have enveloped her, coupled with a nervous dread that kept her continually on edge.

'Raschid has received a letter from Faisal,' she continued. 'Soon he will be returning home, I am sure.'

Felicia shuddered. So Raschid *had* read the letter. Dear God, how was she going to face him? She could not! Excusing herself to Umm Faisal, she went to her room. If only they were still in Kuwait and escape were just a relatively simple matter of presenting herself at the British Embassy. But they were not in Kuwait. They were in the desert. The desert. . . . She looked out across its golden emptiness; perhaps a breath of fresh air might help clear her thoughts.

She went downstairs. Outside Umm Faisal's sitting room she paused, hearing voices. Raschid's voice.

'Rest assured, she will not marry Faisal,' she heard him saying, and her face whitened with pain and despair.

Without knowing how she got there she found herself in the courtyard. The huge wooden gates stood open; the desert beckoned, offering solitude and escape from her agony. Like a sleepwalker Felicia walked through the gates to where the waters of the oasis glittered.

So many small wounds, so carelessly inflicted, all combined to make her heart and body one dreary mass of pain from which there was only one cure—Raschid's love.

CHAPTER TEN

ONE tear followed another down her pale cheeks. She walked on, head down, not comprehending where her unwary feet were taking her, wrapped in her thoughts.

The sun was hot on the back of her neck. Her legs ached and she seemed to have been walking for a long time, but strangely she had no desire to stop. Some instinct beyond her control urged her on. Her blouse was soaked with perspiration and her hair clung damply to her skin. She raised a listless hand to ward off a persistent fly droning angrily next to her ear. Her head felt muzzy, and she was very, very thirsty. She thought longingly of a glass of fresh lime-juice—then she halted suddenly in her tracks and stared back in the direction in which she had come.

She was lost! Completely and absolutely lost. She had broken the first law of the desert. She had wandered away from the sheltering protection of the oasis and no one knew where she had gone.

What was worse, Zahra and Umm Faisal were to visit Saud's mother during the afternoon, and probably no one would realise that she was missing until she didn't appear for dinner! The harsh reality of her plight dispersed the woolly misery clouding her brain. No matter how hard she searched the horizon there was no sign of the oasis—no sign of anything apart from the vast solitude of the desert itself.

She had to sit down because her legs suddenly refused to support her any more, and anyway, wasn't there something about staying put in one place because when you were lost you just wandered round and round in circles, exhausting the body's pitifully frail defences and making rescue harder? Felicia licked her lips and tasted the salt rimming her top lip. Closing her eyes in despair, she remembered the salt tablets she should have been taking. Sickness and giddiness swept her in alternate waves; her eyes ached from the fierce glare of the sun, everywhere she looked an unending vista of sand upon sand.

At length when it finally sank in that she was well and truly lost, she crept into the lee of one of the sandhills hoping the meagre shade it afforded would provide some protection from the sun's dehydrating heat.

Nothing moved. The only creature foolish enough to brave the elements was herself—a pale, singularly ill-equipped female.

Time passed. She slept and awoke, stiff and more thirsty than ever. The world was a molten brass bowl with nowhere for her to escape the burning rays of the sun.

She closed her eyes again and tried not to think of the tinkling fountains in the courtyards. Her tongue snaked over cracked lips. Her throat felt as though she had swallowed the entire Sahara. Had her absence been noticed yet? Without her watch she had no means of gauging time.

Slowly at first, and then with growing fear, she acknowledged that by the time anyone did realise she was missing it could be too late.

She would have cried, but she had no tears left. Sick and exhausted, she tried to crawl a little farther across the sand, but fresh waves of nausea racked her, the landscape swayed unsteadily beneath her feet as her eyes stubbornly refused to focus properly.

She gave a dry sob. She was going to die, alone in this harsh environment, her bones picked clean by scavengers and vultures.

Hysteria bubbled up inside her. Stop it! she commanded herself. Nothing would be achieved by giving way to her emotions. She had no one but herself to blame, and anyway, what pleasure did life hold for her now?

The lengthening afternoon sun threw long shadows across the desert. High above the inert figure on the sand a bird wheeled and hung motionless, a tiny speck in the distance. Its acute hearing, more finely tuned than any human ear, picked up a sound carrying on the clear air and it circled the girl once or twice before winging westward.

Voices impinged upon her consciousness with the imperfect clarity of waves heard from a sea-shell.

Felicia struggled to make sense of what she could hear, but it was too much effort and she succumbed to the desire to close her eyes and keep them closed.

Someone was rolling her over on to her back, touching her skin with hard sure fingers, and she pushed ineffectively at them, wanting to be left alone in her comfortable, pain-free cocoon of nothingness.

She wasn't allowed to, though. Those merciless fingers touched and prodded until she was forced to acknowledge their presence.

'She's suffering from salt deficiency,' she heard someone say, 'and over-exposure. Fortunately she had the sense to keep her face covered. We'd better get her in the Land Rover. . . .'

The Land Rover! She stiffened. The Land Rover was associated with pain, and she had had enough of that, but it was useless, she was being lifted and carried by someone—the same someone who had discussed her so dispassionately—a someone whose identity hovered lazily on the periphery of her awareness. She could feel the rise and fall of the chest against which she was held. It was very comforting to be held thus, and she had a childish desire to remain there, surrendering to the cotton-woolly sensation that made nonsense of her efforts to comprehend what was happening.

'I'll drive, Raschid.'

Raschid! Her contentment splintered into a thousand tiny fragments, and her eyelids flickered open as a small moaned protest escaped her cracked lips.

'It's all right, Felicia, you are quite safe now,' Achmed comforted her.

Safe! Weak relief spread through her. Gone was the

intense heat, punishing her sensitive skin, but still her body trembled with convulsions of reaction she was powerless to control. Of all her senses only those of touch and smell remained unaffected, and through her trembling palms she felt muscles contracting in what she guessed to be tightly reined anger, the scent of male sweat pungently close to her nostrils as the arms holding her tightened fractionally.

Raschid offered her security and she took it gratefully like a tired child too exhausted to reason, her head dropping like a dust-streaked flower too heavy for the slender stem supporting it.

She remembered now! She had wandered out of the oasis because Raschid had hurt her, but her muddled thoughts could not tell her why. She only knew in his arms were peace and safety, a haven for which she had longed all those weary hours in the blistering sun. She closed her eyes and let her senses dictate her actions. Her fingers curled instinctively into the soft cloth of the *dishdasha* beneath her cheek, her breath expelled on a soft sigh as she sought and found the opening which gave her access to the sun-warmed male chest. Unaffectedly she turned her face into it, breathing in the scent of male skin, unaware that above her Raschid's face tightened, a small muscle beating suddenly in his jaw, as he looked down at her passive body.

'Little fool! She could have died out there. . . .'

'She gives you her trust, Raschid,' Achmed murmured, looking from his wife's uncle to the girl lying against him. 'It is a precious gift.'

'She is still unconscious. I doubt if she is aware of anything at all,' was the uncompromising response. His fingers clenched and emotion broke through the barrier of his reserve. 'What possessed her to wander out into the desert? If Nadia had not alerted us. . . .'

'She will tell us when she recovers,' Achmed told him gently. 'Now is not the time for recriminations and lectures. Let us praise Allah that she is safe. Thank God

Zahra and Umm Faisal are still at Saud's. They at least
have been spared the anxiety. Look,' he added, his eyes
on Felicia's face, 'she stirs. She is recovering consciousness.'

Awareness came and went in encroaching and receding
waves. Water splashed down on to her face and she drank
greedily from the flask that was proffered, but she had
barely done more than wet her lips with the life-giving
nectar when it was withdrawn.

'Gently!' a stern voice warned. 'Too much will make
you sick.'

The effort drained her. She closed her eyes and the
world swung away. When she opened them again they
were approaching the oasis. She heard Achmed say
something to Raschid, and then the Land Rover stopped.

Achmed opened the door. They were in the courtyard
of the villa. Nadia came hurrying towards them, her face
breaking into a relieved smile when she saw all three of
them in the Land Rover.

'She is safe?'

'Quite safe,' Achmed reassured her. 'I'll take her up to
her room, Raschid.'

'I'll do it,' was his terse reply.

Felicia felt the bed give under their combined weight.

'Shall I send for Doctor Hamid?' Nadia asked
worriedly.

Raschid was bending over her, and something of her
panic must have shown in her eyes, because he said over
his shoulder, 'No need. It's merely salt deficiency, as I
told Achmed, that and too much sun. I'll deal with it.
You get back to Zayad—I heard him crying as we came
in.'

'He caught our anxiety,' Nadia admitted, glancing at
her husband. 'You must go for Mother and Zahra. They
will wonder what has happened. Thank goodness we don't
have to greet them with the news that Felicia is missing.
It was a wonder that you found her, Raschid.'

'Without the falcons I doubt that I would. She had

wandered miles from the oasis.'

There was silence, and then cool, detached hands were easing her aching body out of the sand-stained garments on to deliciously cool fresh sheets. From the bathroom she heard the sound of running water—a sound she had longed for during her ordeal. She opened her eyes and discovered that Raschid was standing by her bed. Awareness came back on a floodtide. She had gone out into the desert because she had overheard Raschid discussing her with his sister. Raschid had read Faisal's letter! She struggled to sit up and was pushed back against the pillows, Raschid's hands cool against her heated skin.

'You are badly burned,' he told her unemotionally. 'Your skin must be attended to. I would call Nadia to you, but she is too upset.'

'I can manage,' Felicia assured him, knowing that she could not.

For a moment his eyes seemed to darken and then he was walking to the door. Long minutes dragged by while she tried to summon the energy to walk to her suitcase. Surely she had brought with her some anti-sunburn cream? She had small hope of it completely easing the heated burning of her skin, but it might ease the pain a little.

She was halfway across the room when an incredulous oath stopped her in her tracks, as Raschid plucked her up and returned her unceremoniously to her bed.

'What the hell were you doing?'

Tears stung her eyes. She dashed them away, suddenly noticing the tube of cream he held in his hand.

'I was going to the bathroom,' she told him. 'I wanted to have a shower, to comb my hair. . . .'

'You nearly perish in the desert and all you can think of is brushing your hair?' He strode to the dressing table and returned with her brush. 'If I wasn't sure it's too late by a considerable number of years to have any effect, I would be tempted to wield this implement on a part of your anatomy where it might produce better results!'

Her face burned.

'You wouldn't dare!'

'Don't tempt me,' Raschid advised her. 'You've pushed me to my very most limits, Miss Gordon. Believe me, it wouldn't take very much at all to push me over them! Now sit up.'

She did as he told her, conscious of the scantiness of her brief bra and pants, as he methodically stroked the brush through her hair.

The effect was nerve-tinglingly sensual, but he seemed impervious to it, brushing her hair until it fell round her shoulders in a soft bell.

'That is your hair disposed of,' he said grimly, 'but as far as your shower goes, I'm afraid you'll have to forgo that in favour of something a little less exhausting. Stay there.'

He disappeared into her bathroom, and came back with a sponge and towel.

'I want to put some of this cream on your burns, but I think we had better remove some of the dirt first,' he told her.

'I can do it myself.' So this was what he had meant by 'less exhausting.' Felicia shuddered at the thought of having to endure the clinical touch of his hands on her body, when she longed for them to caress her in fierce possession.

He didn't bother to reply, merely pushing her back on to the pillows and disposing of her protests by the simple expedient of ignoring them.

His touch was sure, and strangely relaxing, as he bathed the dust from her tired limbs. There must be something wrong with her, she thought achingly. She was actually enjoying this, even though she knew Raschid felt not a single jot of answering desire. Only when his fingers brushed the exposed curve of her breast did she move, trying to stop the colour rising betrayingly in her cheeks.

Raschid seemed unaware of her tension.

'Soon be finished,' he told her coolly—so coolly that

she replied crossly, 'Yes, doctor!'

His eyebrows rose, as he reached for the tube of cream he had placed on the floor.

'I can manage the cream myself,' she began hurriedly, but the glint in his eyes warned her that she was treading dangerous ground.

'I think not,' he murmured silkily. 'Now turn over, please.'

She knew better than to defy him, so she presented him with a mutely protesting back, hunching her shoulders and burying her face in the softness of her pillow. Nothing happened and she relaxed her tensed muscles, raising her head to look at Raschid. He was regarding her with glinting anger, coupled with another emotion she could not name.

His fingers were cool against her overheated skin, massaging the cooling lotion into her shoulders with a circular movement at once intensely relaxing and yet somehow subtly seductive.

As first she told herself she was imagining the steely determination she had read in his eyes, but as the pressure of his fingers deepened, their subtle message increasing with each punishing stroke, her breathing became more and more erratic as she fought to control the desire pulsating through her. Her brain screamed at her to tell him to stop, but she lacked the willpower. His hands lifted the heavy weight of her hair off her shoulders, his fingers kneaded the bunched muscles at the base of her neck, until the tension eased.

'Turn over, Felicia.'

Her heart seemed to be beating in her throat. She couldn't breathe. She felt his hands slide down to unclip her bra, the weight of his body as he kneeled over her. She closed her eyes, trying to breathe evenly and slowly while she fought for self-control.

Hard fingers slid under her, turning her resisting body. She refused to look at him, glad of the protective darkness of her room. She would not let him see the desire she knew must be in her eyes.

His touch remote, he smoothed more lotion along her burning forearms and neck.

Perhaps she was going mad, she thought hazily. Perhaps she had only imagined the sensuality of those earlier caresses?

Tears welled in her eyes. She lifted her hand surreptitiously to brush them away, but it was pushed away, as Raschid's hands cupped her face, forcing her to meet his eyes.

'Tears?' he whispered mockingly. 'For whom do you shed them, Felicia Gordon?'

'Myself.' One sparkling tear accompanied her forlorn admission, trembling like a diamond against the darkness of Raschid's skin, and then unbelievably she heard him curse, his arms tightened urgently around her, the warmth of his skin a welcome panacea for her bruises, his mouth brushed her face in light, butterfly kisses, teasing and tantalising, his hands returned to cup her face, so that her lips were forbidden the contact they craved.

'Well, Felicia Gordon, am I a substitute for Faisal now?'

Faisal! The letter! But it was too late. Her tears flowed faster, her hands going up of their own accord to lock behind the dark head those tormenting few inches away, pulling him down towards her.

'Please, Raschid!'

Where was her pride? Her determination to keep her love a closely guarded secret? They were gone, swept away in the wild tide of longing that surged through her, destroying the barriers of years. In the darkness her eyes begged silently. His hands moulded the fragile bones of her face, tracing the curve of her mouth which parted involuntarily to press a kiss against their hard warmth.

'Please what?' he mocked, his lips a mere breath away from hers.

All her need of him was in her eyes, giving her the

message her lips could not frame.

Triumph edged the glittering look that swept her from head to foot, but Felicia closed her mind to it, tormented by a yearning desire to know his full possession just this once.

Moonlight silvered her body as she arched closer to him. Her body felt weak with longing, her hands trembling as she reached feverishly towards him.

'Very well,' he murmured at last. 'But be sure you know who it is who possesses your body, Felicia Gordon,' he told her as his mouth feathered across hers. 'Do you know?'

Her mouth dry, Felicia answered his whispered demand with a small nod of her head.

All the promises she had made herself, all the warnings were forgotten. With an inarticulate murmur, she pressed herself against him, and was lost in the punishing ferocity of his kiss, as his lips ceased teasing, and instead swept her into a maelstrom of passion, that left her shaking and vulnerable to the fierce hawk eyes, as they surveyed her bruised mouth and pale face.

Every instinct for self-preservation was sublimated to the desire that swept through her, curling insidiously through her body until a strange lethargy possessed her, and her flesh and bones seemed to melt into the burning heat of Raschid's skin, until there was no part of her he did not know.

His mouth traced paths of fire along her body, drawing from her a response that would once have shocked her to the core. His hands seemed to know instinctively how to teach her pleasure, and his lips followed their erotic journey, until she was pressing feverish kisses against his shoulders and throat, her hands trembling uncertainly against him as she tried to imitate his own skill.

The speed with which he had turned from cool mockery to heated desire reduced her to a mass of quivering nerve-ends, each one receptive to his every breath. Her need to know his complete possession was like nothing she had ever experienced before; wave after wave of a longing so strong that she could barely contain it, surging through her body.

At one point he paused, and she felt a cool shaft of air, followed by the realisation that now nothing separated them apart from her tiny lace briefs. She caught her breath as she acknowledged the full potency of his desire. His knee parted her thighs, his hands sliding over the softness of her stomach and upwards to cup her breasts, before sliding beneath her and lifting her against the hardness of his own body, crushing her against him, as his mouth possessed hers with heated urgency.

Her fingers touched the smooth muscled back. His mouth left hers, descending to the taut fullness of her breast. He muttered something in Arabic, and all at once the wave of sexual excitement she had been cresting crashed downwards, leaving her floundering in painful reality. What was she *doing*? She might love Raschid, but he did not love her. Why was he doing this? Not because he wanted her.

Her anguished protest was ignored, her thrashing attempts to evade his embrace stilled, as hard hands gripped her body.

'Oh no, you don't!' he grated in her ear. 'I don't play games, Felicia Gordon. Did you really think you could lead me on and then not pay the price?' He laughed deep in his throat, a feral sound that turned her blood to ice. 'You may play those games with Faisal, but not with me. And don't tell me you don't want me,' he said softly. 'Your own body betrays you, and anyway it has gone too far now. Nadia is with Zayad; the others will not return for some time. We have all night to spend together, and whether you are willing or not I intend to stay here with you. When the sun rises tomorrow, Felicia, Faisal will never accept you as his wife.'

He turned her to him before she could speak, leaving her in no doubt as to his intentions. What sort of man was he, she wondered incredulously, that he could cold-bloodedly make love to her, just to prevent Faisal from marrying her, especially when all the time he must know that Faisal no longer wanted her?

Her mind might realise the cruelty of what he was intending, but her body still ached for him. Her skin stung in a thousand places from the sun and sand, and she cringed instinctively from the look she saw in his eyes, as he let her feel the full force of his impatient desire.

She could not plead for mercy. Nothing she could say would stop him from pursuing his reckless course. She turned her head, closing her eyes so that he would not see the betraying shimmer of tears filming their jade depths, tensing every muscle against what she knew now would be a bitter defilement of all her dreams. Raschid must know that Faisal did not want her, so why this?

He meant to humiliate her; she sensed it, and bit down hard on her trembling lip as she felt the determined pressure of his thighs, hurting, unyielding.

'Don't play the innocent with me!' he gritted above her, his fingers grasping her hair and forcing her head round. 'Or has my nephew got a fetish about virginity that you pander to?'

Her eyes gave her away, her face bone-white as she flinched back.

Tears streaming down her face, she screamed at him, 'Stop it! Stop it! You know Faisal no longer wants me—I saw the letter. He told me he was writing to you.'

'Faisal no longer wants you?' He had gone very still.

'You know he doesn't,' she accused bitterly. 'I heard you telling your sister that he would never marry me. Because you'd written telling him about my "wanton" behaviour. Is that what this was all about? Another example of my unsuitability to be his wife? Why bother to put yourself out? You've already done enough. I would have been gone from here long ago if Faisal hadn't urged me to spend all my savings.' She faced him proudly with bitter eyes. 'Have I suffered enough to pay for my ticket home, or must you humiliate me further?'

Raschid got off the bed, his back to her as he pulled on his clothes.

'I don't rape virgins,' he told her harshly, turning round suddenly, his face suffused with angry colour. 'What were you thinking of? Has no one ever warned you about pushing a man too far? Think yourself lucky I stopped when I did.'

He turned on his heel, leaving her alone with the shattered fragments of her dreams.

Not until she was quite sure that he would not return did she allow herself to break down, crying until she could cry no more. He had come to her room with one purpose and one only—to deliberately humiliate and denigrate her. Even knowing that Faisal did not want her he had still felt the need to torment and torture her. How he must hate her!

Dawn brought her no surcease from pain. Her heart felt like a lump of lead. How *could* she have thought—even for a moment—that Raschid actually wanted her? How could she have been so stupid? She had allowed her own love to blind her to the truth. Bitterly disillusioned, she contemplated the cynicism with which he had made use of her emotions, playing on them until she was too bemused to know what she was doing. That last painful scene her mind shied away from. Perhaps in time she might be able to re-live it, but not now.

The bedroom door opened and Nadia walked in.

'How are you feeling? I looked in earlier, but you were still sleeping, and Raschid said you were not to be disturbed.'

'How thoughtful of him,' Felicia said tightly. 'But I'm fine. I think I'll get up.'

'Felicia. . . .' Nadia said gently, 'what is wrong? You have been crying. Tell me what is the matter, or I shall go and bring Raschid. Are you not happy with us?'

She could not have hit upon a more effective threat. At the mention of Raschid's name Felicia went white and then red.

'Nadia, I must get away from here,' she burst out desperately. 'If you really do care anything for me, will you help me?'

'To do what?' Nadia asked shrewdly, coming to sit by the bed. 'Return home, or escape from Raschid?'

'Both,' Felicia admitted bravely. 'Raschid despises me, Nadia. Please help me,' she sobbed. 'I can't endure to stay here any longer. . . .'

Weak tears flowed helplessly down her cheeks, as though from some bottomless well, and Nadia's own eyes moistened in sympathy.

'I will do everything I can. I shall go and find Achmed, and ask him to make the arrangements. I am sorry that my family has brought you so much pain, for I see from your eyes that it has.'

'And you will say nothing to Raschid, promise me?'

What fresh, subtle forms of torture might he not dream up, if he knew how she longed to get away? His behaviour last night had not been that of a man with human failings and feelings, but a cold emotionless machine bent on exacting the last measure of payment for the crimes of which he had convicted her. The relentness manner in which he had destroyed Faisal's love for her, the way he had tortured her—they both pointed to a man without pity or compassion, and she had to get away—now—before her pride deserted her completely and she begged him to allow her to stay.

She would have to find Umm Faisal and Zahra and bid them goodbye, Felicia thought wretchedly when Nadia had gone. And then there was small Zayad and helpful Selina, so many people who had touched her heart during her short stay in Kuwait, so much pain when she had to leave them.

She eyed her reflection with distaste. Her hair was all tumbled, her skin flushed from its exposure to the sun. Her body felt gritty with the small particles of sand which had clung to the lotion Raschid had applied. She needed a bath, she decided tiredly, collecting her towel and wrap. Perhaps when she felt clean and fresh she would feel more inclined to tackle her packing.

Although her bedroom possessed a shower, there was only one communal bathroom in the women's quarters, and her footsteps echoed across the tiled floor as she opened the door. The room really was huge, she thought, and the bath positively enormous. She turned on the taps, pouring essence of roses into the water and watching the oil turn the clear water into milky foam.

It felt good to immerse herself in its warm silkiness, and she soaped herself vigorously, as though by doing so she could wash away the memory of Raschid's hands on her body.

The warmth of the water induced her taut muscles to relax, tempting her to linger, soaking in its perfumed embrace.

She never heard the door open, only the decisive footsteps crossing the marble tiles. She glanced up curiously and froze.

Raschid! Wordlessly she clutched the sponge protectively against her breasts, trying to sink beneath the milky cover of the water.

'Why do you want to leave us?'

So Nadia had betrayed her!

'What possible reason is there for me to stay, in a house where I've been abused, reviled, made mock of, tormented. . . .'

'Tormented?' His sharp eyes fastened on her trembling hands.

'Please go, Raschid,' Felicia begged. 'If Zahra or your sister were to. . . .'

'Interrupt us? They won't. They decided to spend the night with Saud's family, and Nadia has been warned not to intrude upon us. To make sure that she does not, I have taken a small precaution.' He reached in his pocket and produced an intricately carved key. 'So you see, my dear Felicia, you are completely at my mercy. Divine justice, one might say. I want to talk to you,' he said suddenly, 'and I cannot do so while you wriggle about in there like a shy fish searching for a lily pad. Besides,' he added sardonically, his eyes resting on the soft curve of her breasts, luminously pale against the water, 'I am quite sure the water must be getting cold.'

It was, but her wrap was on a chair out of reach, and she had no intention of leaving the comparative protection of the bath while Raschid remained in the room.

'If you'll leave me to get dressed, I will come down to your study,' she suggested, avoiding his amused, comprehensive glance.

'Leave you?' Was it her imagination or had his voice suddenly become slightly husky? His glance impaled her, a curious melting sensation running through her bones. In that moment he swooped, lifting her out of the bath and holding her against him, uncaring of the water soaking through his silk shirt, or the shivers that coursed through her as she tried to hold aloof.

'Last night when you denied me I thought you either the shrewdest little bitch I had ever met, or appallingly innocent,' he said suddenly, making her tremble with the swiftness of his attack. 'Why do you want to leave us, Felicia?'

'You know why,' she answered tremulously. His touch was completely impersonal, but she was not going to let him trick her a second time, betrayed by her inexperience into mistaking retribution for desire.

'Do I?'

She trembled convulsively, tears spilling down her cheeks to lie damply against his throat.

His muffled imprecation reached her as his arms imprisoned her. 'By Allah, Felicia. I want you!' he groaned against her lips, stifling her protests. 'I have wanted you from the moment I saw you. Last night when I discovered that Faisal had not touched you I didn't know who I hated the most, you or myself.'

He broke off, as his body shuddered uncontrollably against her, cradling her against him, while he murmured something under his breath. She couldn't move. She was frozen with terror—What was he trying to do? Make her betray herself again? She looked at him, her eyes wild with pain, her expression that of a trapped, tormented animal.

'What do you want?' she whispered in anguish. 'Haven't I paid enough? Just let me go.'

His skin flushed darkly as he looked at her, and she tensed, waiting, dreading what he would say.

'Very well, I will let you go,' he said quietly, 'but only if you listen to me first.'

When she nodded her head slightly he swung her up in his arms, carrying her over to one of the low divans and sitting down with her still in his arms.

'You shame me, Felicia,' he said at last. 'You shame me as no other human being has ever done. When I left you last night I felt sick to my soul, not only for misjudging you, although that was bad enough, but for teaching you to think that I would actually go to such lengths to part you from Faisal.'

'But you said. . . .'

He placed his fingers to her lips. 'No—no more mis-understandings. Let me tell you the truth. Initially it is true that I did want to destroy the love Faisal bore you, for Faisal's own sake,' he admitted wryly. 'He is fickle and too young to settle down, especially with a girl not used to our ways, sophisticated, and perhaps more in love with his wealth than with him. This would not have been the first time I have had to extricate him from such a situation, and shall we say that his track record to date has made me somewhat cynical. But it didn't work out like that. For one thing you were so beautiful, so proud and spirited, and I found myself less and less concerned with Faisal and increasingly determined to make you turn from him to me, at the same time despising myself for being attracted to a woman of the type I thought you to be. I told myself I was a fool, letting your beauty steal away my common sense. But it was my heart you took, driving me mad by coming to life in my arms like the desert after rain, and yet still insisting that you preferred Faisal, I wanted to crush your resistance, to force you to admit that you loved me, but always you eluded me, until at last I thought that you had guessed my feelings for you and were playing on them to make me accede to your betrothal to Faisal. Then I knew bitterness indeed. I admit now that I let my prejudice blind me, seeing only what I wanted to see—what experience had taught me to see. When you walked openly in the street I admit you played straight into my hands, but *I* didn't write to Faisal. I could not bring myself to denounce you to him, much as I longed to part you. When you accused me of knowing that your romance with him was at an end I had no idea what you meant. You see, I hadn't read his letter. While we were in the desert I meant to read it, but there never seemed to be time.' He shrugged. 'To tell the truth, I did not want to read it. I thought he would be begging me to allow him to return to further your romance, and I planned to keep you apart, hoping that you would turn from him to me.

'When I discovered that you were missing. . . . Never as long as I live do I want to go through that torment again. My relief at finding you, coupled with your own stubborn refusal to admit your response to me, drove me over the edge of sanity. This morning I telephoned Faisal and told him that I had received his letter—which I *have* now read. It seems that Yasmin wrote to him after seeing us together in Kuwait, and her letter provided him with the loophole he had wanted. Unlike me he had the wit to see your essential innocence, and he had decided that you would never enter the kind of impermanent relationship he most enjoys. When Nadia came to me and told me that you were leaving I knew I had to stop you. My pride was as the sand beneath my feet. . . . Marry me, Felicia,' he begged. 'I want you now and tomorrow and for all our tomorrows. I want to be the man who will unfasten the one hundred and one buttons of your bridal gown; the one who penetrates the final veil, the one whose child you bear, the one whose grave you share. I want you for my wife, Felicia—my only wife,' he promised. 'Many, many times my sister has pleaded for me to marry, but I could not. Perhaps it is a weakness in me, but I knew always that the woman I married must be the only woman, and when I saw you I knew you were she. Only let me, and I shall wipe away the bitterness of last night and teach you the true meaning of love.'

'But you told me that a marriage between East and West would never work,' Felicia reminded him, not daring to believe her ears.

'Between you and Faisal,' Raschid corrected. 'Because no sooner had I set eyes upon you than I knew that I could never allow you to waste yourself on Faisal, not when I could love you so much better. But you rejected me, and drove me insane with jealousy, tormented by images of you in Faisal's arms, when I longed to have you in mine.'

The ice that had invaded her heart melted, and Felicia looked up at him, giving herself trustingly into his care.

'Tell me you love me, Felicia,' he pleaded hoarsely. 'Tell me I am not deluding myself, misreading what I see in your eyes.'

She knew that this time she was not being deceived and her arms reached out to enclose him, her only protest a small murmur when his breath lost its cool, even tenor, and instead became the charged, uneven rasp of a lover.

Last night had all been a bad dream. Only this was real. There was reverence as well as desire in the sure touch of his hands and lips, as he whispered how desperate he had been when Achmed told him she was leaving.

A small smile touched Felicia's face. Achmed had told

him. So Nadia had not really broken her promise after all. Clever Nadia!

He would never let her go, Raschid whispered fiercely. She would be his prisoner throughout their lives and beyond. They were two halves of an indivisible whole, and Felicia, lost in the wonder of his love, could only agree, her hands running lovingly over the satin smoothness of his back beneath the thin shirt.

'No, not now. . . .' he muttered thickly, trapping her importuning hands. 'I cannot dishonour you.'

'But I want you,' Felicia pleaded,

Strong hands cupped her face, dark eyes understanding and stormy. 'Do you not think I want you?' Raschid whispered unevenly, groaning suddenly as he pulled her against him, letting her feel his need. Her fingers spread against his chest, as she pressed shy kisses against his skin. 'If I take you now, I shall be like a man consumed by thirst, who is given but one sip of water.' He smiled ruefully. 'I have denied myself this long, I can deny myself a little longer, but to taste water now and then have it withdrawn before I have quenched my thirst will drive me to madness. Do you understand?'

If she had doubted the depth of his love, she did so no longer. Shyly she nodded, overwhelmed by the recognition of a need she had never suspected existed; a need only she had the power to arouse—and to assuage.

'It will not be long,' Raschid promised as he removed his shirt and gently fastened it over her. His eyes burned dark with desire as the damp fabric clung seductively to her swelling curves. 'Indeed it must not be long,' he added with a touch of self-mockery. 'My sister already knows of my hopes. Our betrothal shall be announced tonight. I will not give you an emerald,' he told her, betraying his knowledge of the stone Faisal had bought her. 'Do you remember the glass paperweight you gave me?' he asked suddenly. 'Well, I have it still, even though I knew you intended it for another. After you had gone I found it where you had thrown it. I keep it in my room so that I

can always be reminded of you—little though I need to
be. I have slept little since you invaded my life, Felicia
Gordon, but soon I shall know the delights of your love.'

Three weeks later, when the last of the wedding guests
had drifted away, Felicia remembered his words, and
trembled a little as wordlessly he lifted her into his arms
and carried her through the now empty house.

She had begged to spend her honeymoon at the house
by the oasis, and now they were alone, the faint light of
the oil lamps throwing flickering shadows across the
mosaic floor. Outside the Eastern night had veiled the
skies in a shimmer of midnight gauze, studded with
sparkling diamonds, like the tiny buttons fastening her
robe.

Without a word Raschid knelt at her feet, and she held
her breath as one by one he unfastened the tiny fastenings,
pausing only when he reached the last one, to lift the
heavy weight of her hair off her shoulders and remove the
gold necklaces that had been placed there only hours earlier as a symbol of their eternal love. They had had a civil
ceremony too, at the British Embassy, but these were their
real marriage vows that they were to exchange now,
Felicia thought dreamily.

At last she was free, stepping out of the rich fabric of
her robe and walking into the hard warmth of the arms
that opened to enclose her.

'Love me. . . .' Raschid whispered passionately against
her skin as he lifted her against him. 'Love me as I intend
to love you, little dove. Trust me to make the night one of
pleasure as well as initiation. Where there is pain, there
is also pleasure, and there will be pleasure, Felicia. I love
you, my little dove. So very, very much. . . .'

She was gathered up against him and kissed tenderly
and then passionately until every inch of her vibrated with
a desire she made no attempt to hide from him as he
carried her towards the divan and its silk cushions.

Harlequin Plus

DELICIOUS SHISH KEBAB

When Felicia travels to Kuwait, she encounters a host of new experiences, and perhaps not the least of these is the local cuisine. We thought readers might enjoy the following recipe for shish kebab, which is a traditional Arabic dish that in recent years has become popular all over Europe and North America.

Ingredients:
    1 cup dry red wine
    2 medium onions, quartered
    1 clove garlic, crushed
    2 bay leaves
    4 drops hot pepper sauce
    1 tbsp. lemon juice
    ¼ cup olive oil
    2 lb. lamb or round steak, cut into 1½-in. cubes
    1 green pepper, cut into large chunks
    1 tomato, quartered

Method:

Combine wine, onions, garlic, bay leaves, lemon juice, olive oil and hot pepper sauce in large bowl. Add meat, and marinate in refrigerator 3-4 hours or overnight. Remove meat and onions from marinade and place meat on 4 skewers, alternating with onion, green pepper and tomato. Barbecue or broil 10-15 minutes, turning occasionally until all sides are well browned. Serve over a bed of boiled rice.

SUPERROMANCE

Longer, exciting, sensual and dramatic!

Fascinating love stories that will hold
you in their magical spell till the last page
is turned!

Now's your chance to discover the earlier
books in this exciting series. Choose from
the great selection on the following page!

Choose from this list of great
SUPERROMANCES!

SUPERROMANCE

Complete and mail this coupon today!

- -